THE TEXAS COWBOY'S TRIPLETS

CATHY GILLEN THACKER

MILLS & BOON

First Published in Great Britain 2018
by Mills & Boon, an imprint of HarperCollins*Publishers*
1 London Bridge Street, London, SE1 9GF

The Texas Cowboy's Triplets © 2018 Cathy Gillen Thacker

ISBN: 978-0-263-26506-4

38-0618

MIX
Paper from
responsible sources
FSC™ C007454

This book is produced from independently certified FSC™ paper to ensure responsible forest management.

For more information visit: www.harpercollins.co.uk/green

Printed and bound in Spain
by CPI, Barcelona

Chapter One

"Guess my legendary Texas charm finally paid off."

Dan McCabe didn't know how true those words might have been *if* Kelly Shackleford had been in the market for a man in her life. Thankfully for both of them, she wasn't.

Reassuring herself that she was not on a fool's errand, Kelly emerged from her SUV and sauntered toward the irrepressible lawman slash cowboy. Sizing him up all the while. Six feet four inches. Mesmerizing blue eyes. Thick dark hair. A body to die for. And a face so ruggedly handsome it nearly took her breath away.

"What makes you think that?" she asked, stopping just short of where he appeared to be working on extending the height of the fence on some kind of livestock pen. He lifted a fistful of T-shirt and wiped the sweat from his face, giving her an all too brief but tantalizing view of his powerful pecs and taut abs. As the fabric dropped to his waist, she caught a mouthwatering glimpse of the dark strip of hair that arrowed down into the fly of his faded jeans.

He waited until her gaze returned to his eyes before he answered her question with a lazy grin, "You came all the way out to my new ranch to see me."

Desperate times called for desperate measures.

Her heart skittering in her chest, Kelly returned his

flirtatious smile. "You're right. I did," she murmured, regarding him innocently.

Apparently her false cordiality struck a chord in him. A wrong one. He eyed her skeptically. "Any particular reason why?"

She tightened her fingers on her car keys. "You've been saying we should get to know each other better. I've decided you're right." She flushed beneath the intensity of his gaze, took a deep breath, and plunged on. "Becoming better acquainted could be beneficial to both of us." And, more importantly, to others as well.

A brief silence fell, in which she feared that he was going to see her awkward explanation as an open invitation to try to sweet-talk her into the one thing he'd been wanting from her, ever since she had moved to Laramie, Texas, the summer before.

A real date.

"I see." He flashed her an enticing smile. "Is this going to happen before or after you go out with me?"

Kelly tore her eyes from the sensual shape of his lower lip and gave him an exasperated look. "Now, Dan, we've been over that."

She'd fallen hard and fast for a sexy cowboy from a wealthy family once before. Only to be dumped just before giving birth to triplets. No way was she opening herself up to further heartbreak. Never mind with one of the most eligible—and sought after—bachelors in the county.

"We have." He turned and went back to pounding tall metal stakes into the ground on the outside of the existing pen fence, then slanted her a glance over his brawny shoulder. "But never to my satisfaction."

Darn it all, the man was persistent. Not that there was any surprise there. Dan McCabe was a man who was used to getting what he wanted, when he wanted it. The fact he hadn't been able to add her to his growing stable of former "dates" had no doubt frustrated him to no end.

Reluctantly, she moved with him as he worked his way around the perimeter of the entire pen. Then, with a long-suffering sigh, she reiterated what she told him every time the subject came up. "I'm open to being friends."

Finished, he picked up a roll of metal mesh. "So am I, as long as that means we get to go out, too."

When he briefly had trouble attaching the mesh to a tall post with a zip tie, she impulsively stepped in to help him. And just as swiftly regretted it because working together left them in such close proximity.

She swallowed, hard, shook her head, ready to step back. "That can't happen."

He slanted her a glance that was so genuinely appreciative she felt compelled to keep right on assisting him. "Because you work full time," he echoed.

"Yes," she said, drinking in the earthy male scent of him. Why was that so hard to understand? Why did everyone think she needed a man in her life to be happy?

He moved down the line, quickly securing the fencing while she held it against the post. "And are the mother to rambunctious three-year-old triplets."

None of whom he'd met yet.

Aware of the heat emanating from his big, tall body, she said, "Precisely."

He moved a little farther down the line. "And you're not looking for passion. You want love."

"Whoa now." She lifted a hand. Their gazes clashed, then held in a way that had the hot June air between them sizzling. "I never said that."

"Don't have to." Sheer male confidence radiated from

him. "The thing is, I'm not looking for a one-night stand or a casual affair, either."

"So you've said." Unable to decide whether he looked sexier in cowboy clothing or a tan law-enforcement uniform, Kelly continued, reminding him, "Every time you asked me out."

"That is true." He shrugged affably and continued working quickly and efficiently around the last of the perimeter. "It's why I bought this ten-acre property with a family-size home."

And Kelly couldn't help but note that the Bowie Creek Ranch property was gorgeous, with its sprawling ranch house and terrain that was a mixture of rolling grass and woods. "Now all you need is a wife and kids to fill it up. Although—" she turned, looking off into the distance "—I see you've already got a collie." Who was absolutely beautiful. The original Lassie, come to life.

"His name is Shep," Dan informed her.

She squinted to see what the canine appeared to be running around. "And a herd of...goats?"

"Six miniature ones."

She turned so suddenly her shoulder bumped his. Tingling at the contact, she stepped back. "May I ask why?" Having grown up on a cattle and horse ranch nearby, with two parents and five siblings, he likely had enough cowboy in him to last a lifetime. But she had never imagined the tall native Texan to want to be a shepherd.

"Shep is mine. I rescued him as a puppy two years ago when I first moved back here from Chicago. The goats came with the property," he explained. "The family that lived here had to move back to Great Britain for the dad's work, and the goats weren't allowed to go with, so I had to promise to not only find them good loving homes, but care for them until I do."

No surprise there. The McCabes were gallant to the core. "Which is why you're building a fence?"

He sighed. "They keep escaping the pen they were using. As you can see, the original walls are only four feet high. Apparently they need to be at least five feet, so I decided to be extra safe and make it six until I can find them all suitable homes. Then I plan to just take the entire structure down."

That made a lot more sense.

Aware they were at the end, and he no longer needed her help, Kelly stepped back. She gazed at the collie racing back and forth in the grass next to the woods. "Why is Shep barking at that goat?"

Dan grinned proudly. "I trained him to herd them back toward the enclosure. The doe he's chasing is getting a little too far away."

Doe? Kelly squinted. "You can tell the sex from this distance?"

"They're all female." Dropping his tools into the box at their feet, he caught her semi-amused look. "I know. I'm surrounded." His soft laugh was infectious and oh so sexy. "Why, even you…"

Kelly groaned, refusing to let herself be drawn in by his irresistible charm. "Don't start." His constant quips had her smiling and had a way of leading her way off-track.

"So…" A twinkle appeared in Dan's eyes. He let his gaze drift over her in another long, thoughtful survey. "Let me get this straight. You *want* us to become better acquainted, but you *don't* want me to flirt with you?"

Only because of where it would inevitably lead. "No," she said blithely. "I don't."

He took a moment to consider that. Then, seeming to know intuitively she was fibbing about her ever-

escalating attraction to him, he opened the gate wide
and whistled a command to Shep. Immediately his dog
began rounding up the goats and pushing them toward
the enclosure.

Dan turned back to Kelly. Serious now, as he asked,
"So why do you want to get to know me better, if you
don't plan to accept any one of my ten invitations for an
evening out? 'Cause I have to tell you, Kelly, I'm really
not interested in being 'just friends.'"

She knew that, too. Which left her only one option.
Distract—with facts.

"Actually, Dan," she countered, doing her best to put
the brakes on his shameless flirting with a haughty lift
of her chin, "you asked me out *seven* times. Not ten."

"Ah." He stood with his arms folded across his chest
and regarded her smugly. "So you're counting, too." The
corners of his sensual lips turned up.

Darn him for pointing that out!

Kelly ignored what that might mean. With effort, she
met his probing blue gaze. Realizing the time had come
to lay all her cards on the table, said, "I'm here because
I need a favor. And," more importantly still, "I'd really
like it to come from you."

WHATEVER THIS REQUEST WAS, it was serious. And from
the looks of it, highly confidential, as well. "Okay," he
concurred, immediately sobering and calling on the gen-
tlemanly good manners that had been instilled in him
since youth. Aware it was uncomfortably hot outdoors,
he pointed to the house. "Would you rather go inside to
talk?"

Kelly shook her head, looking more beautiful than
ever, and he felt his senses kicking into high gear. It
wasn't just the delicate physical perfection of every inch

of her that constantly captured and held his attention. It was the way she moved—with a kind of sultry, inherent grace. The way her lips curled up softly when she was happy, and the way her chin tilted stubbornly when she was not. She was all energy, all woman. And the slender curves that were hidden beneath a loose-fitting pink cotton shirt and faded jeans—along with her cloud of shoulder-length caramel blond hair and pretty amber eyes—made it impossible for him to look away.

"No. Out here is fine." She rocked back on the heels of her sneakers and peered at him intently, her guard up once again. "But first, I want to make sure whatever I do say to you will be held in the strictest confidence. The same way it would be if I went to a doctor or lawyer or minister."

Disappointment tightened his gut. "So you're coming to me in my capacity as an officer of the law?" He had a miserable sense of history repeating itself.

"No." Kelly shook her head and followed him up to the porch. He walked inside and came back out with two bottles of chilled water.

She accepted one and continued as if he hadn't left. "This is completely *off the record*. In fact—" she paused meaningfully, watched as he uncapped the bottle and drank deeply "—I don't want you to report anything of what I am about to tell you."

Another really bad sign.

Slowly, Dan let the bottle fall to his side. He gave her the kind of once-over he usually reserved for folks who were about to make a terrible mistake. "You understand that I can't be a party to anything criminal," he told her gruffly.

Delicate hand flying to her heart, Kelly took a step

back from him. "Goodness, yes! I would *never* ask you to do anything illegal."

Famous last words, Dan thought, wondering if she had any idea he'd heard them before in a very similar situation. "Or even look the other way if I suspect a crime is being committed," he added brusquely.

Pink color dotting her high, sculpted cheeks, she carefully set the still-unopened water he had given her on the porch railing. "I understand." She ventured closer. "But, on the other hand, if there is a personal problem you could perhaps help with, would you be willing to do that?"

This sounded a lot like his ex. Telling himself there was no way that Kelly could be that conniving, he said, carefully, "I would."

"Good." Her shoulders relaxed. "Because sometimes things aren't what they might seem on the surface."

She looked surprisingly vulnerable now. Subdued. Aware he might have misjudged her—without meaning to—he asked, "Like this conversation?"

Kelly paused for several long beats. Finally, she said, "I have a student in my class I'm worried about."

He squinted at her. "I'm guessing there is a reason why?"

"There is." She paused and took a deep breath that lifted the lush fullness of her breasts. "But I'd rather not divulge that just yet."

As he stood there, inhaling the sweet fragrance of her perfume, he realized he kind of liked her coming to him for help. Assuming, of course, it was all on the up-and-up. "Have you told anyone else of your concern?" he asked kindly. "The school director? Another teacher?"

Her delicate brow pleated. "I spoke with Cece Taylor, another teacher at the school."

"And…?"

Kelly raked her teeth across her lush lower lip. "She thinks I'm overreacting. Which is why I wanted you to come and speak to our two three-year-old classes at the preschool. I know you've worked with at-risk youth, both in your early days at the Chicago Police Department and as a volunteer at the boys' ranch here in Laramie, so I thought if there was a problem with this particular child, you'd be able to spot it."

"Why not just get social services or the school counselor—if you have one—involved?"

"Because," she said, her expression becoming troubled, "then it becomes a whole thing. And if I'm wrong, as I very well might be, then I'm needlessly putting the child and their family through an ordeal that never should have been."

She spoke as if she'd endured a similar contretemps. "Are there any bruises or signs of physical abuse?"

"No." Kelly ran a hand through her hair and began to pace. "Nothing like that. Just…something feels off. And I wanted another opinion." She swung back to face him, more composed now. With a beleaguered sigh, she added, "One not likely to be anywhere near as overly emotional as mine."

His heart went out to her because she really did seem to care about whoever she deemed potentially at risk. He strode closer. "Is it a girl or boy?"

"I'd rather you not know. That way, you won't be predisposed to see something that may or may not be there."

Made sense, he thought, continuing to study her. "You really want to be wrong about this, don't you?" She looked so distressed. He wanted to pull her into his arms and hold her close. Instead, he touched her arm.

Kelly sighed, and just for one second leaned into his touch. "Cowboy, more than you could ever know."

Chapter Two

As Kelly had hoped, the two three-year-old classes at the preschool were completely mesmerized by Dan McCabe's talk on his work at the sheriff's department. With the exception of little Shoshanna Johnson, who never really seemed to get involved in any class activity, they sat raptly gazing at him as Dan explained how law enforcement was there to help them. And how not to be afraid to approach one to ask for help if it was ever needed.

Kelly stared, too, for a completely different…extremely inappropriate…reason.

When he concluded his short but very informative talk, she stepped to the center of the student circle and, studiously ignoring the lawman's sexy, virile presence, took charge once again. "Would anyone like to ask a question?" *And get my mind off just how hot Dan McCabe looks in uniform?*

To her relief, Brian Alderman's hand promptly shot up. "Do you sleep at the station, like the firemen?"

"No." Dan smiled kindly, the glance he directed at Kelly letting her know he realized just how, um, unusually attentive she had been during his speech.

"I live at my ranch," he said, sending another deferential glance her way. Kelly told herself it was the heat of classroom making her sweat. She moved closer to the air-conditioning vent.

"With horses?" Paul Robertson inquired.

A slow smile tugged at the corners of Dan's lips. "Six miniature goats and a dog, actually."

The students appeared perplexed.

"I don't think anyone has any goats as pets," Kelly ventured.

So Dan brought out his cell phone and showed pictures. Kelly relaxed. Maybe, she thought, ignoring the melting sensation in her middle, she would get through this without making a besotted fool of herself yet.

It wasn't that she was attracted to him, per se.

It was that he was so big and handsome and confident-looking, and exuded strength in a hundred different ways that was the problem. A fact he seemed to know darn well, judging by the pure masculine devilry in his smile.

"What are their names?" Sally Baker asked.

Dan put his phone away. "They don't have any."

Moans and cries of dismay followed. "If you have a pet, you have to name it," Teddy Franklin pointed out.

"Point well-taken," Dan said.

Kelly smiled. "Maybe we can think up suggestions later and send them to Deputy Dan."

Excited suggestions followed, while in the middle of the group, Shoshanna Johnson sighed, burying her head in her knees.

"Any more questions?" Kelly said, trying not to worry over her new student's continued lack of involvement.

Another hand shot up.

Uh-oh, Kelly thought, knowing where this was likely to go as Dan turned and called on her triplet daughter. Michelle squinted at him. "Are you married?"

Despite the fact they'd just gone from goats to his

marital status, Dan somehow managed to keep a poker face. "No," he said genially. "I'm not."

"Are you going to be?" Kelly's son Matthew asked out of turn.

Dan flashed a devastating smile. "I hope so."

Kelly could imagine that. There were some men who were just meant to be surrounded by loved ones. Dan McCabe was one of them.

Michelle raised her hand again, and it was all Kelly could do not to groan aloud. "Well, then, can you marry our mommy?" Michelle asked plaintively. "Because she needs a husband."

Michael—the most independent of Kelly's triplets— frowned. Forgetting for a moment what he was supposed to be doing, he stood up and argued back stalwartly. "No, she doesn't!"

Doing her best to stifle a self-conscious blush, Kelly interjected quickly in a desperate attempt to change the subject. "Actually, I have a question for Deputy Dan." All eyes, including the handsome lawman's, turned her way. She noted the amusement in his eyes. "Have you ever been called to help a kitten or puppy in trouble while on duty?"

Dan's masculine confidence lit up the entire room. "Actually, I have." He launched into a dramatic tale that quickly had all twenty-eight preschoolers captivated.

"Nice save," he murmured twenty minutes later when Kelly walked him to the door.

The kids were busy attaching their Sheriff's Star stickers to their clothing with teacher Cece Taylor's help. Only Shoshanna—who was idly inspecting the goldfish in the tank—seemed uninvolved. "Sorry my triplets put you on the spot," she murmured, embarrassed.

His eyes glinted with an indecipherable emotion. "Not a problem."

But there was one. She wanted to ask him if he had come to the same conclusion she had. Aware this wasn't the time to get into it detail, however, she said only, "About what we had talked about a few days ago. Did you notice anything?"

"I did."

Hoping he might have some ideas about what she could do, Kelly asked, "Would it be all right if I phoned you later?"

He nodded briefly, his eyes taking in the thoughtful look Cece was giving them. "Thanks for inviting me to speak." Hat still in hand, he strode off.

Kelly returned to the kids in the classroom. Aware it was time for outdoor play, she and her fellow teacher escorted the children to the playground. Cece's glance followed Dan, who was getting into his squad car.

"Don't," the fifty-five-year-old educator said.

"What?" Kelly asked, even though she already knew.

Cece harrumphed. "Every single woman in town has a secret thing for him." She raised a hand in frustration. "I mean, why not, the man practically took out an ad in the paper when he moved back here, saying Wife and Kids Wanted Immediately."

She turned to look Kelly in the eye, as much substitute mother now as friend. "But he's never going to follow through on that wish. If he were, he certainly would have chosen one of the thirty or so women he's taken out for dinner—or should I say an interview—in the last couple of years. One of my nieces, included."

Kelly knew Dan's reputation with the ladies. He was both gallant to the core and a heartbreaker. "I'm not looking for a husband. Been there, done that."

Cece studied her, accepting that. "Even as a lover, he'd be a bad bet."

"Not looking for that, either," Kelly said.

Even though the sinfully sexy lawman stirred her senses the way no man ever had, or likely ever would.

UNFORTUNATELY, KELLY'S ATTEMPTS to connect with Dan, once her kids were in bed asleep that evening, went to voice mail. Finally, around nine thirty, she was about to give up waiting for a return call when she heard a vehicle pull into her driveway.

She looked out to see Dan emerging from a silver pickup truck that had seen better days. He was clad in jeans, an untucked denim shirt and boots.

Her heart skittering in her chest, she stepped onto the porch of her one-and-a-half-story bungalow before he could ring the bell.

"Sorry it's late," he said. As he neared, she caught a whiff of soap and mint. "My shift ended a little later than I expected."

"You didn't have to come by." Or shower before getting here, either.

He shrugged, affable as ever. His glance drifted over her. "Conversations like this usually go better in person, don't you think?"

He had a point. Even if this was, oddly enough, beginning to feel a little like the beginning of that date with her that he'd been wanting.

Catching a couple coming down the block with their two dogs, she said, "Why don't you come in?"

He followed her inside.

Aware there was less of a chance of them being overheard if they moved to the rear of the house, she led him toward the kitchen, where she had the makings of the next day's school lunches spread out over the kitchen island.

Catching his hungry look, she asked, "Have you eaten?"

"I'll grab something on my way home."

It would be rude not to offer. Especially since he had just done her a pretty big favor with nothing asked in return. "I think we can do better than that." She smiled. "If you are interested in a sandwich that is."

"Actually, if it's not too much trouble, a sandwich would be great."

She layered shaved ham and provolone on wheat, added lettuce and tomato. Then brought out the Dijon and mayo. He chose both, then sat down on the other side of the island. "I'm guessing you are concerned about the thin little girl with red hair."

So he had spotted the issue, too. "Shoshanna Johnson. She moved here a couple of months ago."

Ever observant, he guessed, "And is still feeling a little down about being uprooted to Laramie County, I take it?"

Kelly added cherry tomatoes, carrot sticks and cucumber wedges to the divided lunch containers. She closed them with a snap and slid them into insulated lunch sacks. "That's what the other teachers think."

"But you don't buy that?"

Kelly knew what it was like to be a little kid of a single mom and an only child, at that, who was sad or worried. It really cut deep. But, not wanting to divulge that, she merely said, "Well, a move is always scary and unsettling, especially at that age, but…the preschool is a cozy, safe place, and she's been welcomed by the other kids. The staff has gone out of their way to make her feel comfortable, too." Their hands brushed as she handed him a bottle of sparkling water.

Dan made no effort to move away. "Yet she remains isolated."

"Yes." Hand still tingling, Kelly slid the lunches into the fridge.

Dan surveyed Kelly thoughtfully. "Are there any learning difficulties?"

"No." Because that would have explained a lot, too. "She's able to pay attention, color within the lines, answer questions and follow directions when she wants to."

"And yet...she just usually doesn't want to?"

"That's just it." Kelly handed Dan a package of chips. "Some days she does. She'll come to school with a smile on her face and participate. And other days, it's like she's deeply worried about something, and she remains withdrawn the entire time."

He continued devouring his sandwich. "Any signs of abuse or neglect?"

Deciding it was silly to stand there when he was sitting, Kelly came around the island and took the stool next to him. "None that I can see."

He swiveled so they were facing each other. "Have you talked to her parents?"

Kelly sighed. "Shoshanna's dad died almost a year ago, rather suddenly I understand. I've asked her mom to come in for a parent-teacher conference, but Sharon Johnson keeps rescheduling. Work issues at the auto dealership where she works as the new financial manager, she says."

Dan opened the bag of chips and offered her one. "Think she's avoiding you?"

Kelly took one and munched on it. "Maybe," she said

as the salty deliciousness melted on her tongue. "But maybe she's just settling in, too."

He finished his sandwich, stood and carried his plate to the sink. He looked ready for action.

His brow furrowed. "What would you like me to do?" he asked gruffly.

Besides kiss me?

Flushing, Kelly said, "Be…discreet."

HER REQUEST SUDDENLY had a slightly shady ring to it. One he had heard before. "Discreet," Dan repeated. "As in operating outside the normal rules and regulations?"

She inclined her head. "You have connections. As well as a background as a detective."

Also something he had heard before.

He tensed. "Which means I could do what…in your view?"

She shrugged, the ends of her silky hair brushing her shoulders. "Ask around. Maybe do a clandestine background check…"

Dan's gut tightened.

There were times in his life when he kept waiting for the other shoe to drop. This was one of them. "That's not allowed, Kelly."

She met his level gaze with an indignant one of her own. "Maybe not in an official capacity as a sheriff's deputy," she theorized.

"In any capacity," he corrected sternly, stepping nearer. The fragrance of her hair and skin sent his senses into overdrive. "Unless I want to file a report and go through official procedure." He paused to let his words sink in. "In which case I'd be duty bound to report anything the least bit suspect that I found."

Kelly's face suddenly reflected the concern he felt.

Color flushed her cheeks. "Let's forget it," Kelly interjected quickly, looking sorry she'd ever started down this path. And while that comforted him, he was still worried that she'd been all too willing to bypass ethics. And worse, had wanted him to do so, too.

A long silence fell.

Her worry returned.

He waited until she looked at him. "As I mentioned the other day, if you are this concerned, why don't you just talk to a social worker?"

She scoffed. "Who, if approached, would be forced to open up an official investigation?"

He edged closer, taking in the agitated gleam in her amber eyes and the stormy set of her luscious lips. "And I wouldn't be?"

Calmly, he corrected her mistaken view of Laramie County Department of Child and Family Services. "You can trust social services here, Kelly."

"No." She rubbed the toe of her sneaker across the oak floor beneath them. "You can't." She bit her lip and glared at him mutinously. "You can't trust them anywhere."

Okay, so she was ticked off at him. "How do you know?" he challenged.

She released a short, bitter laugh. "Because I spent *years* in and out of the system."

He paused. "You were a foster child?"

A brief, terse nod. "Off and on, my entire childhood."

She stalked out of the kitchen. He followed, keeping a respectful distance. "What happened?"

She spun around, shoving her hands into the pockets of her knee-length shorts. "It's a long story."

And obviously a very painful one.

He put a consoling arm about her shoulders. When

she didn't continue, he prodded gently, "If you want me to understand where you're coming from, never mind help you, you're going to have to tell me a little more."

She stepped back slightly, so they were no longer touching, and ran her hands through her hair. "My mom was a registered nurse who suffered from cyclical depression. She also developed an addiction to prescription medicines."

Regret pinched the corners of her mouth.

Swallowing, she shook her head, recalling, "So, whenever things spiraled out of control, she would end up in the hospital, or rehab, and I would end up in the system."

No wonder she mistrusted DCFS. "That must have been really tough on you."

"It was." Moisture glimmered in her eyes. "My mom always got better when she underwent treatment, but then she would have to prove that she could take care of me again. And that would take weeks and months of both of us living under the microscope." Kelly sighed. "And then by the time I was finally allowed to be back with her, the stress of maintaining her sobriety would send her spiraling again." Kelly compressed her lips miserably. "I'd have to hide it and pretend nothing was wrong. I knew if I didn't I'd be taken away from her again. And it was awful."

Dan pushed aside the need to pull her into his arms and asked gently instead, "Where is she now?"

"She died of an accidental overdose five years ago."

This time he did reach for her. "I'm sorry, Kelly."

Standing stiff as a board in his arms, Kelly nodded.

He let her go, stepped back. "Do any of your coworkers know this?"

"No." She met his gaze and didn't look away. "The

only reason I'm telling you is so you'll help me make sure that Shoshanna isn't grappling with a similar heartache."

He took her hand in his and turned it palm up. "You really believe something is going on with that little girl?"

Compassion lit her pretty amber eyes. "I really do, or I wouldn't have come to you."

"Then," Dan decided, just as seriously, "there is only one thing we can do."

Chapter Three

When Dan arrived at Kelly's home Saturday morning, she'd had plenty of time to reconsider their hastily made plan.

"You're sure this is a good idea?" she asked, stepping onto the front porch. Luckily, they had a few moments to talk since the triplets were inside, putting on their socks and shoes. A task that always, no matter how much of a hurry they were in, seemed to take at least ten minutes.

Dan stood with one brawny shoulder braced against a post. In a short-sleeved polo that brought out the azure blue of his eyes, jeans and boots, his short hair neatly brushed, and the barest hint of stubble on his handsome face, he looked like any dad out to do weekend errands with his family.

Except he wasn't her husband or the triplets' daddy... He gave her an appreciative once-over, too, and flashed a reassuring smile. "Think of it as an unofficial welfare check on a neighbor we may or may not have good reason to be concerned about. Besides," he said as he pushed away from the post and came to stand next to her, "it will be fun for your kids. The county auto mall is having a huge Father's Day sale the entire month of June, and every dealership is participating. The open house today is supposed to feature some great deals. The showroom is air-conditioned. Most kids really like looking at all the different types of cars on display."

Kelly frowned and ventured a look inside, to see her kids still dawdling over their task. Knowing that asking them to hurry would only slow things down considerably, she sighed and swung back to him. Why did he have to be so handsome? And inherently helpful?

Using her nerves as a shield against her attraction, she frowned. "There will also likely be salespeople bent on making a sale to me."

His eyes tracked the downward curve of her lips. "So?"

Aware it was that kind of interest that had her heart racing, she pointed out, "I'm not in the market for a new vehicle. My SUV is only three years old."

He stepped up to the storm door, peering into the house, too. Seeing the kids sitting on the floor, making little progress, he grinned cheerfully, waved and called in, "Hey, buckaroos, hurry up!"

Miraculously, the triplets began to move faster.

"Luckily, I am looking."

For what? Love? She tabled the ridiculous thought.

"Are you serious?"

He braced his hands on his waist. "Yes. I've just been waiting for this sale since it sports the best prices of the year, across all makes and models."

Kelly surveyed the vehicle at the curb. His truck did look like it was on its last set of tires.

"Then why aren't you going alone? Since you have a valid reason."

He tucked a strand of hair behind her ear. "Because I don't know Sharon Johnson and wouldn't have a reason to talk to her. Since her daughter Shoshanna is in her class, you do."

True, but… "You could always ask her out on a date," Kelly pointed out, wondering what that gentle touch of his would feel like elsewhere.

He dropped his hand. "Cute. No. There's only one woman I have my eye on right now."

A delicious shiver of anticipation swept through her, but for all their sakes, Kelly pushed it away. "And she's not about to date you." She referred to herself in the third person, too.

Smug satisfaction radiated off him. "We'll see."

Behind them, the screen door banged open. To her relief, Michelle, Michael and Matthew came barreling out. "Deputy Dan!" they cried in unison.

"Hey, kids." He hunkered down to greet them in turn. Giving out high fives and low fives all around. "'Bout time you buckaroos came out to say hi to me."

"We couldn't," Michelle explained. "Till we had our shoes and socks on. Mommy said."

"What are you doing here?" Michael asked a tad suspiciously.

"I'm shopping for a new pickup truck or maybe a large SUV. I'm not sure. Your mommy has agreed to advise me."

"What's 'vise?" Matthew asked, tucking his hand in Dan's.

Michelle took his other.

"Advise me means to tell me which one is best," Dan explained patiently.

Michelle rolled her eyes as she skipped down off the porch. "That's easy, Deputy Dan! The pink one."

Michael latched on to Kelly. She placed her hand on his shoulder. "I don't think they make pink SUVs," Kelly said.

Michelle harrumphed. "Well, they should."

"No, they shouldn't," Michael disagreed.

And they were off.

Since Dan was going to need his pickup truck to get a trade-in price, and all the safety seats were in her SUV, they both drove to the auto mall.

As planned, they parked at the dealership where Sharon was the new financial manager.

As Dan ambled over to help the triplets onto the ground, she couldn't help but think what a good daddy he would make one day.

Assuming he ever chose a wife, that was.

Given his recent "one or two and done" dating history, it seemed in doubt.

Inside the air-conditioned building, couples and families milled about. The triplets, who had never visited the inside of a showroom, were in awe of all the shiny new vehicles. "Wow," they breathed in unison.

Behind them, a man approached. "Going to get Daddy a new car or truck for Father's Day?" he said.

Dan and Kelly and the kids turned to face him. "Whoops. Didn't recognize you from the back," the gung-ho salesman said.

Dan extended his hand. "Hey, Pete."

"And who is this lovely lady?" the salesman asked. "And three adorable kids?"

"Kelly Shackleford. Her triplets, Michael, Matthew and Michelle."

"Deputy Dan is going to be my mommy's new husband," Michelle announced. "'Cause she needs one."

Kelly blushed bright red.

"I see," Pete said.

Bored, Michael looked up at Dan. "Can we climb inside one of them?"

"Check out the eight-passenger Suburban." Pete

walked over to open it up. "Perfect for the man with a big family." He winked.

While the kids scrambled inside, Pete launched into a spiel about features. Kelly looked around. She'd only met Sharon Johnson a few times since the single mom generally used the car pool lane drop-off to leave and pick up her daughter from school.

"So what's your time frame for buying?" Pete asked as the kids climbed into the rear row and practiced sitting and looking out the windows from that perspective.

"Most likely the end of the month," Dan replied. "I'm in no hurry."

They talked about competitors.

"What about financing?"

"Sharon Johnson's in charge of that. Actually, here she comes now." Pete waved her over.

Guilt at more or less spying on another single mom filled Kelly. Halfway there, Sharon was waylaid by the dealership's sales manager. Kelly couldn't make out what was said, but she could tell it wasn't welcome news. Sharon appeared to be first taken aback, then upset.

Dan gave Kelly a look. Was this it? Work stress traveling from mom to child?

Sharon's mouth tightened, and her face went from almost white to beet red. Kelly didn't stop to think. Seeing another woman in need, she moved across the floor to interrupt what appeared to be a pretty thorough semipublic dressing-down. "Hey, Sharon!" she said, moving in to give the stunned woman a warm hug. "How great to see you today!" She moved back to address the white-haired sales manager. "I don't believe we've met, though."

"Walter Kline." Abruptly turning on the charm, he shook Kelly's hand. "Glad to have you out here today."

Another salesperson approached, a sheaf of papers in his hand.

Walter glared at Sharon, a look even Kelly could read. "Figure it out," he snapped, turned on his heel and strode away.

"Everything okay?" Kelly asked.

Sharon sighed and ran her hands through her short, perfectly coiffed auburn hair. "I only have a sitter until noon. They just told me I have to be here until closing or later."

That was definitely a problem, and one Kelly fully sympathized with. "Could I help? Maybe pick up Shoshanna, take her to my place for a playdate?"

Sharon paused. "I don't want to impose."

Kelly waved away her concern. "We single moms have to stick together."

Dan ambled up to join them.

Sharon shot him a curious look. Briefly, Kelly made introductions. "So you're the sheriff's deputy who spoke at the preschool," Sharon concluded.

Dan nodded.

"You made quite an impression. Shoshanna told me all about your rescue of the two kittens caught in the hole in the trunk of that tree. And, of course, your herd of miniature goats."

Dan grinned. "It was an easy crowd to impress."

Beginning to relax, Sharon grinned back.

From across the showroom, Walter Kline glared at them impatiently. Sharon stiffened. "Let me know if you have any questions about financing options," she said, loud enough for others to overhear.

"I will," Dan promised.

"Me, too," Kelly said, though she had no intention of buying a new vehicle at this time.

Sharon headed off. "I'll call my sitter."

She and Dan collected the kids from the interior of the family-size SUV. "Can we get this car?" Matthew asked excitedly.

"It's cozy." Michelle sighed.

"I like our old one," Michael countered. "It's red!"

"So do I," Kelly said.

In fact, her whole life was so cozy and complete right now, with her kids, nice home and job, she hated to rock the boat by changing anything. Never mind bring someone new into it. So what if she didn't have a love life? In the past, romance had ultimately brought her nothing but unhappiness, so she was better off without that complication.

Much better off.

Although, she couldn't help but admit having Dan as a very good platonic friend, spending time with him on weekends, hanging out, kids and all, held a definite appeal.

"Want to meet somewhere for lunch after you pick up Shoshanna?" he asked as they walked out to their respective vehicles.

Kelly decided a little adult company while she supervised four kids might be nice. "Why don't you come by my place?" she asked. "I'll whip something up." She figured she owed him that much.

"Sounds good."

They left the dealership. Shoshanna had already talked to her mom about the change in plans and, looking intrigued by the possibility of a playdate with her preschool classmates, went willingly with Kelly back to her home.

Which made Kelly wonder.

Was Shoshanna without friends or an opportunity to make any outside the school day because her mom was

working such long hours? Could that be part of the little girl's unhappiness, too? Guiltily, Kelly realized she
hadn't done much to welcome the child to Laramie outside the school environment.

She could do better, as well.

"So you think that's all it is," Dan said. He had returned
to Kelly's house, and the four kids hit the playroom while
she bustled about the kitchen, putting together a quick
meal. "You think Sharon is worried about keeping her
new job and Shoshanna is picking up on that?"

Although they were out of earshot, Kelly had a good
view of the children. They were getting along nicely
and having fun, so she began to relax. "I had the feeling Sharon's boss might fire her if she didn't comply."

Dan kept an eye on the kids, too, as he moved back to
watch her add chopped celery and apples to the chunks
of roast chicken already in the mixing bowl. Quietly, he
reflected, "Sadly, that wouldn't surprise me. Walter Kline
is not from around here. He came in when the family that
owned the place for years sold it back to the automobile
maker's corporation. From what I've heard around town,
he's putting enormous pressure on all the salespeople."

Kelly whipped together a mixture of plain yogurt,
lemon juice and honey. "So Sharon came here for a more
low-key life than she had back in Houston, and ended up
in what could very well be worse straits."

She watched Dan turn to look at Shoshanna, who was
trying on some of the dress-up clothing. Big floppy hat,
heels, a long strand of pearls and some clip-on earrings.
Michelle had on her favorites—a pint-size princess gown
and jewel-encrusted crown. Both girls were grinning and
preening before the play-mirror. "Sharon's little girl sure
seems happy and engaged today."

She did, Kelly noted in satisfaction.

Dan hung around for another hour. Long enough to partake in chicken salad sandwiches, and chips and fruit. Then help with the cleanup as the kids retired again to the playroom, this time to build structures out of wooden blocks. Shoshanna was smiling and talking as readily as the triplets.

"Feel better?" Dan asked.

Kelly hung up her dish towel to dry. "I do." Maybe she'd been projecting some of her own childhood fears and troubles onto the child.

She watched Dan drain the last of his iced tea. "It's possible she just needs time to adjust. And more of an effort from me and some of the other moms to include her in activities after school hours."

She walked him to the door, realizing how much this felt like a date, albeit a family one. Resisting the urge to step in and give him a big hug for fear how that would be seen, she smiled instead and said, "Thanks for asking me to go today. I feel a lot more at ease."

"Good." He grinned at her with a tantalizing sparkle in his eyes. "Maybe now we can go on that date you owe me."

Owe! Kelly drew herself up to her full five feet nine inches. "I don't remember promising..."

His low chuckle sent another shimmer of awareness drifting through her.

He caught her hand and brought it to his lips. "I stand corrected." He bent his head and lightly kissed the back of her knuckles before lifting his head to look into her eyes. Murmuring playfully, "But it's only fair, don't you think? That you give me a chance to woo you?"

Feeling her knees begin to quiver, and wondering what

the impact would be like if he really kissed her, Kelly repeated the old-fashioned term in surprise. "Woo me?"

He rubbed his lips across her knuckles even more seductively this time. "Mmm-hmm."

Aware how easily this man would be able to seduce her, she jerked her hand away. Sent him a deadpan look from beneath her lashes. "I'm not woo-able."

He stepped back, his hearty chuckle hanging in the sizzling air between them. "Famous last words."

Were they?

Was she woo-able after all?

"But," he allowed patiently, still holding her eyes, "if that is true, then you have nothing to lose, do you?"

"You have a point," Kelly countered just as mildly. Although, she thought in amusement, maybe it wasn't the one he was trying to make. "There's only one way to put an end to your current quest." Only one way to prove to him that she had already failed at matrimony once and wasn't about to give it another go.

The meaning of her words sinking in, his eyes radiated pure pleasure. "Give me what I want?"

"Once," Kelly stated. So he would see what she already knew, that she was not "the one" for a marriage-minded man like him.

He could then put her in the Rejected Candidates column. Move on to the next female hopeful. And she could put this crazy, ill-conceived attraction she felt for the sexy husband-wannabe behind them.

WEDNESDAY NIGHT Dan stopped by his sister Lulu's Honeybee Ranch to pick up a gift en route to his date. The petite dark-haired spitfire looked him up and down. "Aren't you all fancy!"

He stayed a good distance from the hives where she had been working. "It's just a shirt and jeans."

Lulu stripped out of her protective white bee suit, hat and gloves. Surveyed him with a wry smile. "Ironed shirt and jeans. Shirttail tucked in. Your good brown leather boots. Freshly shaven and showered, smelling of after-shave, and did you also get a haircut by the way?"

He grunted. "It was time."

"Mmm-hmm." Lulu rolled her eyes. "Who's the lucky lady this time? Must be someone special if you're going to this much trouble."

"Kelly Shackleford."

His sister did a double take. "Well, what do you know, stud. The pretty preschool teacher finally agreed to go out with you?"

With way too many stipulations.

Dan nodded, happy after months of trying to have gotten that far. "She has."

Lulu's eyes narrowed. "On a school night?"

"She was only able to get a sitter from seven to nine."

"Where are you going?" Lulu led the way into her ranch house.

"The concert in the town square."

Another pitying glance. "Your choice or hers?"

"Hers," Dan allowed.

A smirk. "That'll be nice. And public."

Beginning to lose his temper, Dan groused, "What's your point?"

His only sister sobered. "I'm just saying Kelly's put a lot of safety nets into this outing. Weeknight. Setting with a lack of intimacy or privacy. A short overall time period and early end."

Put that way… "You're saying I should read something into this?" Other than the fact she'd been so eager to go out with him she couldn't wait until the following weekend?

"Aren't you?"

Hell, yes. Unfortunately.

The irony wasn't lost on him, either.

He'd spent a lot of time going out with women he suspected might be all wrong for him, just to be sure he wasn't missing out on a chance to get married and have a family. Now that he finally felt differently about a woman from the outset, she was preparing to simply go through the motions with him in order to officially eliminate him as a viable romantic prospect.

Much to his chagrin, there was no denying the universal payback of that.

Lulu gently patted his arm. "Want my advice?"

Lord knew he really appeared to need it in this case. "Always."

Lulu handed him a gift set of four kinds of honey. "Make every second count, cowboy."

Dan planned to.

UNFORTUNATELY, THE MINUTES were ticking away before they even got started.

Kelly's teenage babysitter was late and had not arrived yet. The triplets—who had been sent to let him in the door—were thrilled to see him yet very unhappy he was taking their mother out.

"It's not fair," Michelle pouted. "We wanted to go to the park, too."

Dan was trying to figure out how to handle that when Kelly came breezing down the staircase in a burst of flowery perfume.

Damn, she was gorgeous. Her full-skirted sundress

hugged her torso, accentuating her full soft breasts and slender waist. She was still fastening her earrings.

She accepted the four-pack of Lulu's famous Honeybee Ranch honey from him with thanks and a smile. Set it aside. Then turned back to her daughter, her caramel-blond hair flowing over shoulders, explaining gently, "I told you. Dan and I aren't going to the part of the park where the playground is. We're going to the bandstand to listen to music."

"But I like music!" Michelle folded her arms in front of her and pouted all the more.

"Are they going to sing 'Farmer in the Dell'?" Matthew wanted to know. "Or 'Hokey Pokey'?"

"No," Kelly said firmly. "In fact," she said levelly, with a telltale look Dan's way, "I'm pretty sure it's all very boring music. Isn't that right, Deputy Dan?"

Getting her cue, he nodded soberly. "I think your mommy is right. You all would be really fidgety if you had to sit through that for two whole hours."

"Well, then," Michael declared, independent as always, "I don't want to go."

A knock sounded.

Kelly opened the door and Tessa Lowell came in, hair still wet and smelling vaguely of chlorine. Briefly, introductions were made. "Sorry, Ms. Shackleford," the sitter said. "The swim meet ran late, and I couldn't leave until I got my ribbon."

"I completely understand," Kelly said.

Dan looked at his watch. It was nearly seven thirty. "Any chance you could stay until nine thirty then?"

"No problem." Tessa grinned.

Kelly looked like she wanted to interject. Then grabbed her shoulder bag instead. "You know where all the emergency numbers are."

"I do. But not to worry, Ms. Shackleford." Tessa beamed. "We're going to have even more fun than you-all are!"

"Walk or drive?" Dan asked as they hit the driveway.

He'd waited for this moment for so long, he could hardly believe his good fortune. Kelly seemed to be having a similar "is this really happening after all" moment.

With a shrug, she tilted her head at the clear blue sky with a few scattered white clouds. "Well, it's not that hot or humid. Parking along the town square can be hard to find, and," she said, drawing a breath that lifted and lowered the enticing swell of her breasts, "it's only four blocks."

He fell into step beside her. "Then we walk." He debated whether to take or hand or not. Decided not. "You look pretty tonight."

"Thank you. So do you." She shook her head. Tried again, more succinctly this time. "I mean you look *handsome*."

He grinned. "Good to know." And deep down it delighted him that she was obviously as acutely aware of him as he was of her.

She swung to face him. The sexual vibe between them intensifying, she raised a cautioning hand. "I know I agreed to do this, Dan. But—" her lower lip took on a rueful curve "—I think it may have been a mistake."

Chapter Four

"A mistake?" Dan had been ready for this kind of reticence, given how high Kelly had her guard up. But he hadn't really expected it until the end of the evening. He reached over and took her hand in his, wondering all the while what it would take to make her feel as crazy with longing and giddy with desire as he did at this instant. "Why is that?"

Color swept her cheeks. "Because I know that you're looking to settle down and get married."

He stepped even closer. "And?"

She kept her eyes on his a disconcertingly long time. "I'm not marriage material," she evaded finally.

It wasn't the first time she had told him this. He hoped it would be her last. "Who told you that?" he scoffed. "Your ex-husband?" If so, he'd like to wring the jerk's neck.

Her teeth raked across the soft lusciousness of her lower lip. "How do you know I'm divorced instead of widowed?"

"I figure if you'd already been married to the love of your life and didn't want to date for that reason, you'd just say so. Plus, there would likely be photos of the triplets' daddy around the house. There aren't. At least not that

I've noticed. Or some mention of him, either from you or the kids."

She retreated into scrupulous politeness. "I might have never gotten married at all."

He wasn't surprised to find her still holding him at arm's length. Slanting her a sidelong look as they began to stroll in the direction of the town square, he noticed how the dwindling sunlight caught the shimmer of blonde in her caramel hair. "Was that the case?"

Another shadow crossed her face. Their eyes locked, providing another wave of unbidden heat between them. "No."

Dan savored her nearness and the pleasure that came from being alone with her. "How long after you had the kids did you divorce?"

She shoved her hands in the pockets of her skirt. "It became final one week later."

One week? He let his glance drift over her slender form to her spectacular legs. "After giving birth to triplets?" He couldn't hide his astonishment. His gaze returned slowly to her face, pausing on her lips before returning to her long-lashed amber eyes.

Sadness came and went in her guarded expression. "It's a very long story."

"We've got at least three more blocks."

She sent him a quelling look.

"More," he added, curtailing his own rising emotions, "if we take the long way."

Kelly smiled faintly. Sighed. "Okay, maybe you should know."

Now they were getting somewhere. He studied the mixture of regret and longing in her eyes.

"I didn't date when I was younger because of how chaotic my life was, so I was pretty naive when I met Grif right after college. I had a lot of student loan debt, so I was working weekdays at a preschool and then moonlighting on weekends at his family's real-estate firm in Phoenix." She took a breath. "Grif had just graduated from Wharton Business School, and he felt entitled to a bigger role in the family company. His parents wanted to see him married—to someone of an appropriate social standing—and settled down with kids first, before they gave him a part-ownership in their multimillion-dollar enterprise."

Dan caught her hand in his, and this time she didn't let go. "That didn't go over well?"

Kelly sighed and looked down at their entwined fingers. "No. He quit working for them, took a job with their biggest competitor and eloped with me."

"He was using you?"

Kelly's jaw tautened. "To tick them off, yes." She stared straight ahead.

"Did you know that?"

"No." She frowned. "He was so charming I thought he was wildly in love with me. I probably would have gone on thinking that, at least for a while, had I not become pregnant right away. His family went ballistic. And when we realized I was carrying triplets, so did Grif."

Curtailing his rising anger, Dan guessed, "He didn't want the babies?"

"Of the child of an addict who spent half her life in foster care?" She smirked derisively. "No. So they sent the family lawyer to see me with a proposal. If I would not claim the children were legally Grif's, they were prepared to set up a very generous general welfare trust that would provide for me and for the children, through college. All I had to do was agree to an uncontested divorce, pretend to the few people who knew about the pregnancy that I'd miscarried, leave Arizona immediately and settle elsewhere."

"What would happen if you didn't agree?"

"They were going to fight me for custody. And they promised me it would be very unpleasant. They'd bring up my unstable childhood and my family history of addiction. And with their money and influence, they might have won." She released a pensive sigh. "So to spare my children that kind of ugliness, I said yes to their plan, agreed to an uncontested divorce and chose Texas."

Dan hated the way the bastards had treated her. He was also glad they were permanently out of her life. "So Grif's name isn't on the triplets' birth certificates?"

"I left the space blank."

He saw the good and bad in that, too. Extricating their hands, he wrapped his arm about her shoulders and drew her closer. "Have the triplets asked about their father?"

Their paces slowed. "Only in a general sense."

His protectiveness toward her grew. "What did you tell them?"

She leaned into him, her voice soft. "That they were my very own little miracles, sent from heaven so we could be a family."

So true.

"And that not all families have daddies, or mommies, for that matter." Her voice caught slightly. Embarrassed, she averted her gaze. "And it's okay, as long as children have at least one parent who loves them." She swallowed, composing herself, as their steps slowed even more, then stopped. "And I do love them, very much."

"You're a wonderful mom, Kelly." He grasped her shoulders, and turned her to face him.

She sighed with a mixture of sadness and frustration.

"And yet, I can't give them what they should really have had all along. A complete family."

Maybe not with her ex-husband. But there were other possibilities, too.

He searched her face, not really all that surprised by the depth of her concern. Or his. Kelly and the triplets were fast filling the empty corners of his heart. Gruffly, he observed, "Don't be so hard on yourself. Your kids are all doing great."

With a faint smile, she tipped her face up to his and conceded cautiously, "For now, yes, because so far they've accepted my version of events. Although—" she inhaled sharply, looking worried again "—as you noticed, Matthew and Michelle are fixated on my finding a husband." Another even longer, more heartfelt sigh. "That way, they figure, they'd have a daddy."

"Michael…?" Dan prodded.

Kelly made an exasperated face. "Also wants a daddy. But he *doesn't* want me to have a husband."

"Complicated."

Kelly lifted her eyes heavenward before finishing wryly, "Oh, yes, my life is most definitely complicated."

As was his. Now that she and her kids were in it.

"And it's about to get even more complicated," Kelly fretted as they resumed walking once again.

"Because…?"

Dan turned the corner with her, aware if they went any slower they'd soon be going backward. He didn't mind. He was in no hurry to get to the concert, either. He much preferred simply spending time with her.

Kelly turned her gaze back to his and lamented softly, "In two weeks, the preschool is hosting the Father's Day picnic. And I know all of these questions, and more, are likely to come up then."

KELLY DIDN'T KNOW why she had confided so much in Dan. Usually, she kept her personal feelings about things locked away inside. But there was just something about being with the big, strapping lawman that made her feel it was okay to let down her guard a little. Enjoy life again.

"So who knows about what you've gone through?" he asked with the trademark McCabe compassion.

Kelly pushed away the desire roaring through her and forced herself to respond rationally, "The entire story? Here in Laramie? Just you."

His blue eyes filled with understanding. "What does everyone else think?"

If she strained to listen, she could hear the sounds of the concert in the distance. Kelly turned to look up at him. She knew it was reckless, but the romance-starved part of her did not want their time alone together to end.

"They think," she said, "that I had a brief, unsuccessful marriage in Arizona to a man who decided he did not want children, and because of that, I have sole custody of my triplets."

Giving her no chance to protest, he drew her back into his arms. "Why did you tell me?"

She drew a breath. And, knowing they were possibly on the brink of even more heartache, forced herself to look into his eyes. "Because," she said softly, pragmatically, "I can see how interested you are in me. Or think you are, anyway. And I don't want you to be left with the impression that any of this is going to go anywhere."

She saw the indecipherable emotion flash briefly in his eyes and plunged on. "I owed you a date because you helped me set my mind at ease about Shoshanna. And…"

He lowered his head to hers and delivered a kiss. Short, sweet and utterly seductive.

"What was that for?" Kelly gasped, so dizzy it rocked her world.

He rocked her world.

Dan grinned and kissed her again. A little more slowly and deliberately this time. "Because," he responded tenderly, "I didn't want you to have to wait until the end of our date to stop fooling yourself and realize I'm not the only one feeling something here."

IT WAS JUST one embrace. One short, sweet, incredibly tender and evocative embrace. Yet Kelly couldn't stop thinking about it and remembering just how wonderful it had felt to be caught up against Dan McCabe's tall, strong body.

And she was *still* thinking about it two hours later, after the concert ended, when he was walking her home. As well as thinking about how to phrase what she knew she had to say.

When they were one street away, she took an enervating breath and began. "You know how we agreed to just one date…?"

His eyes crinkled at the corners. "I recall you wanting to limit it to that."

Kelly swallowed, already tingling all over. "Because I thought that, if, at the end of our night out, either one of us just wasn't feeling it." Or shouldn't be feeling it. "Then…"

He stopped walking abruptly, caught her hand. And looked deep into her eyes. "Except, Kelly, I am."

With a great deal more difficulty than she imagined, she ignored his soft, sexy declaration and pushed on as if he hadn't spoken. "…the two of us might decide we would be better off as friends."

Just as he had done with the dozens of other Laramie County women he had dated.

To her consternation, he rejected the notion, again. "Or friends and more," he murmured persuasively, lowering his head.

She barely had time to catch her breath, and then he was pulling her all the way against him, kissing her again. And again, and again. Inundating her with so many sensations at once. The hard warmth of his body. The delectably minty and masculine taste of his mouth. The clean masculine fragrance of his skin. Heavens, the man knew how to kiss. How to make her want and need and feel, how to draw her into the promise of more, so much more, before letting that same kiss come to a slow and oh-so-sensual end.

When he finally pulled back, he rasped, "I don't think we were meant to be 'just friends.'"

Her body didn't think so, either.

Frazzled, she moved a slight distance away from him and propelled herself forward, in the direction of her home.

With difficulty, Kelly reminded herself that it was a man only half as charming as Dan who'd broken her heart before. Could she really go through that again?

The common sense side of her said no, she could not. "Well, I do," she countered stubbornly, folding her arms in front of her.

He fell into step beside her, matching her step for step as she hurried home. "Okay," he said.

Kelly spun on him, echoing in disbelief, "Okay?"

It didn't help that the sky was velvety black now, with a brilliant quarter moon and a sprinkling of stars. Or that the warm summer air was blowing gently over them. The town streets just as quiet and deserted and serene as they had been before the concert.

Dan shoved his hands in his pockets as they rounded the corner. "We don't have to agree on everything, Kelly."

That soothed even as it disturbed. "Meaning you won't pursue me?"

He offered her his killer smile and gave her a lazy once-over before returning ever so deliberately to her lips. "I didn't say that. Exactly."

She ignored the low insistent quiver in her belly. Resolved not to let him know just how much he was getting under her skin, Kelly huffed, "Then what *are* you saying?"

He delivered a slow, heart-stopping smile. "That you might need some time to think this over before you officially deem us 'one and done.'"

She wished he would quit behaving like the conquering hero, quit fueling romantic fantasies that had gone too long unexplored. She didn't need him to remind her—with every request for a date—what a rut she had been in. Didn't need him to charge past her carefully built defenses. Or make her realize how lonely she had been for just this kind of companionship. She looked at him defiantly when they reached the street lamp on the next corner. "Just so you know, cowboy, I'm not going to change my mind."

His eyes were dark and unwavering on hers. "Okay."

She swallowed. "Okay you believe me?"

"Okay." Chuckling, he tugged her close and dropped a string of kisses along her temple to just behind her ear. "I'll let you reserve the chance to change your mind."

She splayed her hand across the center of his chest, pushed him away and kept right on walking. Marching, really. As quickly as she could. "You really are the most maddening man!" she called over her shoulder.

So much so that if it were Christmas, he would have to be put on the naughty list.

He caught up with her on the sidewalk in front of her home. "And you're the most maddening woman. But you don't see that discouraging me, do you?"

Kelly swung around to face him. She trembled at the raw tenderness in his gaze. She had the strong sensation—or was it hope?—that he was going to kiss her again.

And that she was going to kiss him back...

He moved toward her. She moved toward him. And just before their lips met, an excited rap on the windows of her home captured their attention.

In frustration, Kelly pivoted to see all three of her children with hands and faces pressed against the living room windows. Tessa standing behind them.

Dan laughed. "Quite the welcoming committee."

No kidding. Kelly muttered, "They're supposed to be asleep!"

The front door opened. The triplets and their sitter came barreling out. "You're back!" Michael noted happily.

"Hi, Deputy Dan!" Matthew said.

Michelle asked, "Did you get married yet?"

"No," Dan said with a wry chuckle.

Michelle pouted. She placed her hands on her hips. "Well, when?"

Never, Kelly wanted to say. Given how much Dan McCabe had turned her life upside down in just what, a matter of three, four days? Making her want and need and feel. Instead, she said, "It's past your bedtime. Why aren't you all asleep?"

Three shrugs. Tessa apologized. "Believe me, I tried, but they couldn't settle down tonight."

Kelly knew why. She hadn't had a date with anyone since they'd been born. So this was definitely a new situation.

"Well," Dan said, reading the situation correctly. "I can see you have your hands full…"

'Say good-night to Deputy Dan," Kelly told her children.

"Good night," they chorused, gathering around the handsome lawman for a group hug that was just as warmly returned.

"Night, kids." Dan looked at Kelly. "I'll call you tomorrow." Grinning and whistling, he sauntered to his vehicle.

In an aside only Kelly could hear, Tessa said, "Wow, he is hot!"

Very hot, Kelly thought, still tingling from all the kisses she had received and the one that had been interrupted. Not that it would make a difference. She had already made up her mind which way this was going to go, and it wasn't into anything romantic—and potentially heartbreaking.

WHEN KELLY ARRIVED at school the next morning, she had a message that the director, Evelyn Winters, wanted to see her. "What's up?" she asked as she entered the senior administrator's office.

"We've been getting a lot of positive feedback on the talk Dan McCabe gave to the three-year-old classes. The kids were enthralled with the photos of his miniature goats, and the idea of naming them, too. Assuming that was a real suggestion and not just a misunderstanding?"

Kelly knew better than to throw anything out there, even casually, since preschoolers were very literal.

"The kids wanted to know the names of his goats, and he didn't have any, which was upsetting to them, so

I mentioned that maybe we could all think about coming up with names for them. I was thinking it might be something to do on a rainy day."

"So you weren't serious?"

Kelly hedged. "He's planning to rehome the herd as soon as possible. He just hasn't found places for them yet."

Evelyn clapped her hands with enthusiasm. "All the more reason to put the goats on the ranch field trip next Monday, then."

Kelly blinked. "What?"

"We've already got horses, cattle, alpaca, sheep and chickens for them to go see. Pet goats would be a nice addition."

Pushing the memory of their recent kisses out of her mind, Kelly swallowed. "I'm not sure Dan McCabe would be up for that." *Me, either.*

The director waved. "I know his family, and I have a feeling he wouldn't mind. In any case, I'd like you to ask. And if he says yes, you'll also need to drive out to his ranch and work out the logistics of having the buses on his property, safely unloading the children and so on."

Kelly gulped. "Today?"

"Yes. I'll even take your class for a couple of hours if you can arrange to do it this afternoon so we can get it on the permission slips going out tomorrow afternoon."

"FEEL FREE TO SAY NO," Kelly said blithely when she got Dan on the phone.

"It's no problem."

Darn.

"But I can't meet you out at Bowie Creek Ranch until around six this evening."

Yet another problem. She gave him another opportunity to bail. "Well, that's the thing. I'd have to bring all three kids."

"It would give me a chance to show them around. You, too, actually."

Kelly rubbed her temple. Why were the fates conspiring against her? Tempting her repeatedly with something she knew she could never have? Not for long, anyway.

And it wasn't just she who would be getting hurt here. Her kids were already becoming attached to him.

Oblivious to her worries, Dan said, "In fact, plan on having dinner out here, too."

Yet another objection eradicated.

"And we'll make a night of it."

Exactly, Kelly thought as her heart sped up even more, what she was afraid of.

Chapter Five

Kelly wasn't sure how Dan had talked her into having a light picnic supper at his Bowie Creek Ranch when all she was trying to do was put distance between them. But as she drove out to his place after work, her three tired and soon-to-be cranky kids in tow, she knew the social engagement would also serve an important purpose.

Right now, the sexy lawman had no idea how challenging and time-consuming it could be to take care of three preschoolers. If he experienced that firsthand, maybe he would realize how impossible the reality of dating her was and be less insistent about pursuing her. And then she wouldn't have to worry about fighting her ever-growing physical attraction to him.

"Does everyone understand the rules for tonight?" she asked as they neared his ranch.

The triplets finished their snack of graham crackers and juice boxes. "We have to be good listeners!" Michelle said.

"Say please and thank you, and like whatever he has for dinner," Matthew chimed in.

With a beleaguered sigh, Michael asked, "But what if we don't *really* like it? What if he makes broccoli? Or something yucky!"

In her rearview mirror, Kelly saw faces of disgust

all around as their most loathsome vegetable was considered.

Dan had promised her something kid friendly for the triplets without her even asking. In case he missed the mark, however, she advised, "Then just pretend. And I will feed you something later when we do get home. We are not going to be at the ranch long, in any case. So you shouldn't have any problems minding your manners. Got it?"

"Okay, Mommy!" they chimed in unison.

Though Dan had only a ten-acre spread, his sprawling new ranch house and an old barn were set well back from the rural country road. Three acres or so of pasture and wooded area were located at the rear of the buildings. The remaining seven acres formed a buffer between the ranchhouse and the road, and on either side. Kelly followed the picturesque lane to the oversize parking pad where his battered pickup truck sat. By the time she had turned off the engine and emerged from the vehicle, he was coming out of the goat pen, empty feed bucket in hand.

In jeans, a white twill shirt and boots, he looked handsome and relaxed as could be. He gave Kelly a long, welcoming look that had her quivering inside and out, then turned to the real stars of the evening.

"Hey, kids!" He turned on the outside spigot, then threaded the hose through the links to start filling the long, low water trough. With the water still running, he strode toward them.

"Deputy Dan!" the kids shouted.

A dog approached. The black, brown and white collie had his tail wagging and seemed as happy-go-lucky as his master. Dan put his hand on his dog's collar, and motioned Kelly and the kids over. "Want to meet the Bowie Ranch dog? He's six years old, and his name is Shep."

"He's older than us," Michelle pointed out.

"And he loves to be petted," Dan said as they all took a turn stroking his dog's long silky coat.

Plus, he was sweet and adorable and kid friendly as could be, Kelly noted, pleased.

When he'd evidently had enough affection, which took a couple minutes, the dog collapsed on the ground at his master's feet. Dan rose, giving Kelly another long, lingering look, then grinned down at the triplets. "Ready to go see the goats?"

"Yes!" They pumped their arms enthusiastically and cheered. Together, they set out.

Kelly had made the kids wear light cotton shirts, their summer-weight jeans and Western boots to protect them from insect bites or pesky weeds, but she soon saw she needn't have bothered. Dan had mowed the entire area since she had last been out there.

He stopped just short of the six-foot-high wire enclosure with a hinged gate. Inside, the black and white mini goats had already finished eating and were milling about in the shade provided by a partial canopy. Michelle counted the animals. "Look, Mommy! There are six of them!"

"Can we go inside?" Michael asked.

"It's probably best if you view them from here," Dan said. "Especially since they just ate. But if you put your hands along the outside of the fence, like this—" he demonstrated how to put their open palms on the outside of the chain link, facing the goats "—they'll probably come close enough to nuzzle you."

Matthew's brow furrowed. "What's nuzzle?"

"Put their noses close enough to touch and sniff."

The kids did as asked, then smiled broadly as the cute little black and white animals approached.

"Any chance they could get nipped?" Kelly asked a little nervously.

Dan shook his head. "No. They're gentle as can be, and they're used to being around little kids since the previous owner had them, too. But they can get a little rowdy if they get excited, so it's probably best we do it this way, at least at first."

Kelly agreed.

While the kids stared at the goats, chatting and observing, Kelly turned back to Dan. He was so easygoing and kind. It would be so much easier to avoid him if he weren't. "I think I've seen everything I need to see." Basically, that the ranch was a safe environment. "Do you have any questions for me?"

He sobered, in much the same way he had before he kissed her. "How many kids are coming on this field trip?" he asked, eyes crinkling at the corners.

Kelly tamped down her awareness. Not easy, when he was so tall and powerfully masculine. So very easy to lust after. "There will be four classes of three- and four-year-olds, or sixty-four total. With eight volunteer chaperones, all parents, including Mirabelle Evans—" her nemesis "—and four teachers."

He nodded. "How many buses?"

"Two." They pivoted to discuss where the buses could park, and then safely and easily turn around to drive off the Bowie Ranch property.

The next thing they knew, a metal latch clanged behind them. The gate was wide open and, to Kelly's horror, her triplets were inside the enclosure with the goats, squealing with delight. The goats moved in close, eager for attention. Dan's dog followed, barking and racing around. The children giggled and stepped back slightly, too afraid to do much petting, as the goats began to romp and play with rowdy abandon.

All too quickly, it seemed, the situation was way out of control.

In unison, Kelly and Dan rushed toward the pen, just as Michelle looked down in dismay and let out a piercing scream. "My boots! Oh, no, Mommy, my boots!"

DAN HAD BEEN warned by his friend Clint McCulloch how hard it could be to take care of three-year-old triplets. But he hadn't realized until this moment, with all three children stepping in fresh goat droppings, how hysterical they could be.

"Oh, gross!" Michael said, hopping around, smearing and smudging it everywhere.

"Is that poop?" Matthew asked, holding up his foot and reaching to explore.

"Don't touch it!" Kelly ordered, rushing into the enclosure, as the goats—hearing the raw command in her voice—rushed to the opposite side.

Dan pointed to the opening. "Shep, out!"

His dog, who now had his own paws covered in poop, promptly exited.

By now, Michelle was sobbing uncontrollably. Matthew had ignored his mother's entreaty and had grabbed some poop anyway, and was lifting it toward his nose. Not about to wait to be rescued, Michael was reaching for the hose.

"It's stinky!" Matthew said.

Exasperated, Kelly picked up her son by the waist and carried him out of the pen, then set him down in the grass. Following suit, Dan hoisted Michelle and Michael, retrieved the garden hose and brought it back around to

Matthew. "Let's rinse this off, buddy. Then we'll go inside and get some soap."

Michelle resumed crying. "My pretty pink boots are all yucky."

An understatement if there ever was one.

Kelly knelt in front of her kids. More calm preschool teacher now than exasperated mom. "Let's get these off you." Looking down at her own boots, which were also soiled, she eased those off too.

Noting the goats were still watching from one side of the pen, Dan went back to shut and latch the enclosure. His dog, who had been racing about the small woods at the rear of his ranch, came back and barked at him once.

He understood. Shep was upset.

He didn't want him frightening the kids.

"Quiet," Dan said.

With what seemed like a doggy sigh and frown, Shep sank down onto the grass, and with another loud sigh of frustration propped his chin on his front paws.

Dan turned back to Kelly, as glad for her matter-of-fact attitude as he was chagrined at the mess, and his part in it. If he hadn't been so busy lusting after her, the mischief probably wouldn't have happened. "Why don't you take the kids inside the ranch house to wash up, and I'll handle rinsing off the boots."

"Okay. Thanks." She paused, looking up at him. The twin spots of color in her cheeks made her even prettier. "Sorry about this." She turned to her children with a disciplinary frown. "These three were *supposed* to be good listeners."

The triplets looked as if they were sorry.

They were just little kids, after all. Who were curious as could be.

"No problem," Dan said. And he meant it.

He was just glad he'd been there to help out.

He couldn't imagine how Kelly had done all this on her own for three and a half years.

By the time he had retrieved the antibacterial soap from the barn, and a scrub brush, and cleaned all five pair of boots, Kelly and the kids were properly cleaned up themselves and lined up on the front porch, watching.

Michael pointed out, "You've got icky brown stuff on your shirt."

Dan looked down at the brown stripe marring his formerly pristine white shirt. "So I do," he drawled. Talk about impressing the ladies. Or in this case, lady. One gorgeous, elusive as could be lady.

"It's nasty," Matthew noted, wrinkling his nose.

Kelly tried not to laugh, but Dan didn't bother. His chuckle prompted hers, and their eyes met.

One day, he assured her wordlessly, this would be a very funny story, even if right now they were still in the thick of things.

Her gaze gentled, and he felt the urge to haul her in his arms and kiss her all over again. Maybe take her into his shower, and get them both clean. An erotic fantasy that might have been possible, had they been without their little chaperones. But they weren't, so...

Meanwhile, Michelle's lower lip thrust out petulantly. "I hate stinky stuff!" she declared with fresh insult. "And now it's on my pretty pink cowgirl boots." A fresh tear rolled down her face.

Kelly put a hand to her forehead as if warding off a major migraine. "Kids," she warned, suddenly sounding almost defeated.

They fell silent.

Michelle continued to cry soundlessly.

Dan knew, even if Kelly didn't, this was a time for her

to lean on someone, and that someone was going to be him. He said in a strong, commanding voice, "First order of business is I'm going to wash up. Then, I will show all four of you how we make our boots look brand-new!"

KELLY COULDN'T HELP but be impressed as Dan sat and showed them how to buff their cleaned boots with a soft brush. Now it was time to take damp strips of old T-shirt material, smear them with baking soda and then rub that on their boots. They followed up by rubbing down the footwear again with damp cloths, then wiping with more clean soft strips of old T-shirt material. As she watched him work, his large hands moving expertly over the leather, it was hard not to wonder what those same palms would feel like, stroking over her body.

"So what do you say?" he asked when everyone had finished, his strong male presence like a port in the storm. "Do they pass the smell test?"

Everyone sniffed. Including the very finicky Michelle. She smiled. "No poop."

"None here," Michael said.

"Or here," Matthew agreed.

All three of her kids gave Dan an adoring look. He gave them one back in return.

He was going to be such a good father one day, Kelly thought wistfully as once again their eyes met and held... And she felt an even stronger urge to explore and further their connection.

Luckily, she had her three kids to keep her rooted firmly in reality.

"I'm starved!" Michael declared as they all went back inside his ranch house—this time to have the dinner Dan had promised them. "What are we having?"

Dan's eyes lit up. The familiarity and ease between

them all deepened. "Come and see for yourself," Dan answered with a welcoming grin.

As they moved through the spacious downstairs with its open floor plan, Kelly couldn't help but note how lovely—and almost empty—his abode felt.

Aside from a kitchen table, which looked like it had come from a small one-bedroom apartment and sat in the breakfast room, and an L-shaped sectional sofa, entertainment center, and a desk, the downstairs was pretty sparse. She took in the brisk masculine scent of the soap he had used to wash up. Watched the broad muscles strain against the white cotton of his shirt and remembered how it had felt to be enveloped in their seductive warmth. Realized how much…albeit foolishly…she wanted it to happen again…

Hunger pains forgotten, Michael eyed the staircase. "Can we go up there?" He pointed to the second floor.

"Sure," Dan said, the tenderness and compassion in his eyes, surprising her. "Although," he allowed with an affable shrug of his broad shoulders, "there's not that much to see."

Before Kelly could get out a protest, her sock-clad kids were racing up the carpeted stairs. She hurried after them, while Dan brought up the rear. "Sorry about this," she said over her shoulder.

He waved off her apology. "It's fine. I kind of like seeing and hearing them in the place. Gives me an idea what it will be like one day."

Kelly nodded.

Heavens above, could the guy get any dreamier?

Too bad she wasn't looking for anything long—or even—short term.

They hit the second floor, and she went down the hall in search of her kids. They were running in and out of what looked to be a lot of empty bedrooms. At the end of the hall was the master suite. Dan's bedroom, where a very nice king-size bed dominated the space, and windows overlooked the ranch.

"Wow. You have one big house," she said.

"Six bedrooms, Mommy!" Matthew shouted.

"No seven," Michelle corrected.

"There were six empty ones," Michael announced.

Kelly turned to Dan.

"The previous owners had six kids," he explained, "so they built a seven-bedroom, seven-bath home."

"It is very nice."

"Thanks. I need some help decorating it and filling it up, though."

"I'm sure you'll find someone to help you do that."

He looked into her eyes a long time. "I'm sure I will."

He was *not* talking about us, Kelly told herself firmly, though for some reason her heart fluttered wildly at the mere thought.

"Kids, downstairs!" she commanded when things got even more rowdy.

They raced to the kitchen. "Bet Michael's not the only one who's hungry," Dan mused.

How right he was, Kelly thought. They were all starved, though not necessarily just for food. Affection, for one thing, was often in short supply, with the exception of the mother-child kind.

Dan brought out a bag from the local café-bistro. "So what do you say?" he asked, looking very much at ease as the kids clamored for seats. "PB and J sandwiches, or turkey and cheese?"

After the kids made their selections, Kelly and Dan ate what was left. It was a very family-friendly time. So much so that Kelly began to wonder if she should reconsider her decision to stay single… Certainly, her kids seemed to really like having a man around. Almost as much as Dan seemed to like hosting them?

By the time they had finished their fresh fruit cups, the fireflies were out. "Can we stay and chase them, Mommy?"

Although Kelly yearned to stay, she also knew she had lived in fantasy world long enough this evening. Gently, she told her kids, "We really need to get home."

"Just for a few minutes!"

Dan wordlessly lobbied on the triplets' behalf. There was only so much fighting Kelly could do, especially when he was standing there, looking so ruggedly handsome. "Ten," she found herself saying out loud. "And I'm timing you!"

"Yeah!" The kids raced out into the yard.

Shep approached. He stared at Dan a long time, as if trying to tell him something, then lay down on the back porch with another long, defeated sigh, watching the kids, too.

She paused to pet his dog, then took a seat on the swing. "This is really lovely out here."

He settled beside her and draped his arm along the back of the swing. "So are you. And—" he inclined his head toward the activity in the yard "—the three of them."

She sucked in a breath, aware things were about to get intimate again. She turned toward him, her knee brushing his denim covered thigh. "Dan…" she warned, a thrill rushing through her.

"I mean it, Kelly." He covered her hand with his own. "I've really enjoyed getting to know your kids and having you-all here."

Amazed at how right it felt to be there with him like

this, she looked down at their entwined fingers. Then back up at him. Much more of his inherent kindness and gallantry and she'd fall head over heels for him. "You can say that after tonight?" she challenged playfully. "When they were at their absolute worst?"

The corners of his sensual lips curved upward. "Exactly. If that's all they've got," he said, chuckling, "you've got nothing to worry about."

Except, Kelly thought, she did.

Her growing feelings for him.

Afraid if they stayed any longer, she'd end up kissing him again, audience or no audience, she disengaged their hands and stood. Waved the kids toward her.

They came, reluctantly. Warmth flowed upward from her chest as she turned to face him and prepared to bid him adieu. "Thank you for a wonderful time."

Tenderness filled his eyes. "Thanks for coming," he said, his head drifting slightly lower.

Kelly had the sharp sensation he was about to kiss her again—or would have, had it not been for the hand she splayed across his chest.

Their little chaperones approached. "Mommy, can we say goodbye to the goats?" Michelle pleaded.

When she hesitated, Matthew promised, "We won't go in there this time."

Anything to get them off this back porch, out of the intimate setting and away from the knowledge of what it would be like if she had someone to share her life with.

Kelly drew a quelling breath. "Ask Deputy Dan."

Amenable as always, he said, "Let me grab a flashlight and we'll go."

Together, they trooped around to the front of the house. Shep trotted along with them, looking a whole lot happier now. When they reached the pen, Dan held the light aloft in an unobtrusive way, so they could see the mini goats, but not hurt the animals' eyes.

This time, all three children counted the herd. "One, two, three, four." They paused, as the realization sank in. Matthew turned and said, "Mommy, how come there are *four* goats in there now and not six?"

Chapter Six

Dan surveyed the landscape around them, already quietly and calmly contemplating a plan to retrieve the animals. Although he should have been angry about the missing livestock, he wasn't, Kelly noted. A fact that only added to his allure.

Dan scrubbed a hand over his face. Exhaled. "This was probably what Shep was trying to tell me earlier. He knew they'd gotten away. And there was so much going on—"

"—no one else noticed."

Part of Kelly wished the handsome bachelor would lose his temper, at least a little bit. If he had more faults, it would be easier to keep the barriers around her heart. Instead, he was good and kind to the depths of his soul.

She gathered her children around her and stepped closer to him, peering up into his face. "I feel horrible. What can we do to help?"

His confident gaze met hers. She had the overwhelming sensation he wanted to reach out and comfort her. But didn't. Which was good, because as powerfully drawn to him as she was, she was still afraid of getting too close.

"Nothing, really." He rested a gentle hand briefly on her shoulder, then turned to soothe the kids kindly, "Shep and I will find them."

Her body tingling from the brief contact, Kelly stepped back. As much as the reckless side of her might yearn to explore their attraction to each other, she knew the cautious side of her—the side that finally had her life in order—would not allow her to do anything to disrupt or endanger her family's hard won happiness and serenity.

And that was a good thing. Wasn't it? Especially since her kids' hearts were involved now, too?

"Are the other goats lost, Mommy?" Matthew asked.

"It's dark," Michael fretted.

And getting darker by the minute, Kelly observed,

"And scary out there." Michelle looked frightened, too.

"Not for them." Dan hunkered down to explain. "Animals can see in the dark a whole lot better than humans can. I bet my two runaway goats think they're on a *big adventure*."

Grinning, the kids ruminated on that.

Dan gave each of them a quick, reassuring hug. "There's nothing for you to worry about," he promised. "Everything is going to be fine."

Kelly hoped so.

Otherwise, she'd never forgive herself, and she knew the kids would feel awful, too.

She shepherded the children toward her SUV. Dan helped her strap them into their safety seats.

Although it had been the last thing on her mind when she arrived, it was imperative now. "Call me?" she asked.

He looked her in the eye, protective and take-charge in the way she had always yearned for a man to be. "I will," he promised in a husky timbre that sent a thrill down her spine.

Resisting the urge to kiss him, she got in her car and drove away.

The triplets talked about the goats all the way home. And

they were still worrying about them when Kelly tucked them into bed. "Can you call Deputy Dan, Mommy?" Michelle asked, her little brow furrowing. "Ask him if he found them yet?"

Kelly imagined the strapping cowboy out in the countryside with Shep at his side, flashlight illuminating their way. "He might be a little busy." And had she not had to take her children home, she would have been right there with him.

"Please, Mommy…"

Sighing, Kelly decided it wouldn't hurt. She retrieved the phone from the charger in her bedroom. No sooner had she punched in his number than her phone chimed. Kelly looked at the caller ID. *Dan McCabe*. Thank heaven! "Hello."

His gruff voice rumbled in her ear. "Found them!" he declared victoriously. "They're home, safe and sound."

Had she been there, she would have given him a big, celebratory hug. Relief soaring through her, she said, "Let me tell the kids."

They cheered the news.

"Where were they?" Kelly asked.

Dan grunted. "That's the bad part. In my next door neighbor's vegetable garden. They ate all Mrs. Weller's tomato plants."

Dismayed, Kelly splayed a hand across her heart. "Oh, no," she said softly.

Three little heads popped up from their beds. "What happened, Mommy?" Matthew asked.

Figuring her children might as well learn what not following the rules had wrought, she said, "Dan, I'm going to put the kids on speakerphone. Can you tell them what you just told me?"

"No problem."

"Was the neighbor lady mad at the goats?" Matthew asked when Dan told them where the livestock had been found.

As Kelly hoped, Dan was both direct and truthful. "Yes," he said matter-of-factly. "Mrs. Weller was upset."

"Can we replace the plants?" Kelly, who knew very little about gardening, asked.

"I told her I'd do it for her Saturday morning." The smile was back in Dan's voice. "You're all welcome to come along and help, if you like."

More kudos for the intuitive lawman. "Then that's what we'll be doing on Saturday morning." Kelly held up the phone. "Say good-night to Deputy Dan, kids."

After they had, Kelly asked Dan if he could wait while she delivered another round of good-night hugs and kisses. He could. That done, she shut the door and walked out into the hall and headed for the privacy of her master bedroom. She set the phone, which was still on speaker, on her bed. "I'm so glad you were able to find them," she said.

She could almost hear his relieved smile. "You and me both."

Used to multitasking, Kelly tugged off her shirt and jeans. Her bra went too before her pajama top slid over her head. "There is one more thing." Her voice was slightly muffled as she pushed her arms through the sleeves.

"You okay there?" he asked.

There was no way she was telling him what she was doing. Even if the idea of conversing with him while half-naked was a little thrilling in a very unexpected, naughty way. "Um, yeah." Deciding her pants could wait until the conversation ended, lest she get tangled up again, she sat down on her bed.

"I just need to ask," she continued a little breathlessly,

picking up her phone. "Given what just happened with my kids… Are you still willing to host the field trip?" She leaned against the pillows, imagining what it would be like to host him *here*. With both of them disrobing, getting ready for bed…snuggling beneath the covers… making love…

"Absolutely." Oblivious to her unexpected—and completely inappropriate—romantic fantasy, Dan said, "But this time the pen gate will be sporting dual latches with attached locks."

And hence childproof. Not that it should be a problem with all the teachers and parent chaperones there, watching over the children.

Kelly lounged against the pillows, the phone in her hand. "Good to hear." She paused, thrilling at the thought of seeing him again.

Forcing her mind back to business, she said, "You'll still need to sign the releases, though."

Dan's voice dropped another husky notch. "No problem. I can drop by the school tomorrow."

"Look forward to seeing you," Kelly murmured back, then, before it got any more intimate or seductive, ended the call and resumed getting ready for bed.

As she found her pajama pants and tugged them on, she thought about all she had learned about him during the course of the last week. He was not only gallant to the core, but amazing with her kids, as well as persistent, playful, and physically irresistible. In fact, she'd never met a man that strong or kind or masculine. Never met someone so destined to be a dad. And a good loving one, at that. It was no wonder every woman in town lusted after him! Dan McCabe was a true catch who wanted marriage.

Had she wanted the same thing…

But she didn't.

It was best she remember that.

"SHOSHANNA, DARLING, don't forget to put your lunch bag in the cubby," Kelly reminded gently the next day.

The girl turned, frozen with a combination of guilt and anxiety. Oh, dear. "Did you forget it?"

The three-year-old's lower lip trembled.

Kelly hunkered down in front of the preschooler and gave her a reassuring hug. "That's okay. It happens to all of us. I'll call your mom. We've got plenty of time before lunch for her to bring it to you." And if that couldn't happen, Kelly would share some of her own since she always brought extra for just this situation.

Shoshanna nodded, her eyes glittering moistly.

Kelly motioned to her own daughter. "Michelle, do you and Shoshanna want to be classroom buddies this morning?"

Michelle took the girl by the hand. "Sure. Come on! Let's go play with the dollhouse!"

Shoshanna brightened, and the two girls skipped off. As they did, Kelly couldn't help but notice something else. Shoshanna was wearing the same turquoise-and-white-striped T-shirt and shorts she'd had on the day before. They still bore the same mustard and dirt splotches, so they hadn't been washed.

Had she not followed her mother's instructions when she'd gone off to get dressed that morning?

Or was there some sort of neglect at play here?

Kelly tamped down her suspicions.

And made the call.

Two and a half hours later, Sharon came into the classroom, holding a Cowgirl Café lunch sack, instead of the usual insulated child's lunch bag with petunias all over it. She was walking stiffly and trying not to show it.

Seeing her mom, Shoshanna jumped up from the table, where she working on an art project, and ran over to greet her. The two hugged fiercely, the raw emotion between them palpable. To Kelly's surprise, since Shoshanna usually did not have trouble separating from her mother, the little girl seemed loath to let go, even when Sharon walked back with her to take a look at her coloring.

"It's beautiful, honey. Why don't you finish it so you can bring it home later, and we'll put it up on the refrigerator."

The two hugged one last time, then Sharon moved toward the door. She paused to give another long look at her child. "Is she…tell me she isn't wearing the outfit she had on yesterday!"

Kelly couldn't lie. "I think so."

"Oh, dear. I got an urgent work call when we were getting ready this morning. I'm going to have to pay more attention."

"Hey. Happens to all of us. One minute they're ready, wearing exactly what they're supposed to be wearing. And then somehow when we get where we're going, nothing matches."

"Well," Sharon said, shaking her head, "at least I'm not the only one with that problem!"

"Would you like to stay and observe a little bit?"

She shook her head in regret. "The only reason I could come now is my manager is at an off-site meeting. But I would like to talk with you about something, if I could."

Kelly nodded. She stepped just outside the open doorway, so she could still keep an eye on her class. Sharon seemed to stumble slightly as she moved through the open portal, to stand opposite Kelly.

Instinctively, Kelly reached out a hand to steady her. "Are you okay?"

Sharon winced again. "Actually, no, I'm stiff and sore as can be. I've been trying to alleviate job stress with yoga at night, after Shoshanna is asleep. I did too hard of a workout last night—" she seemed in pain as she shifted positions again "—and I'm paying for it this morning." She laughed softly and shook her head.

Kelly joined in, commiserating. "I know what you mean. I've been known to overdo it a time or two in my regular daily exercise routine myself." Sharon rubbed her shoulder. "Fortunately, it's nothing another dose of acetaminophen and a heating pad tonight won't fix."

Relieved to know what had caused upheaval in her student's household that morning, Kelly smiled again, prompting, "So what's up?"

"You were so kind last Saturday, helping me out with childcare. I wanted to repay you by babysitting the triplets for you, via a playdate at my house for all four kids. Unfortunately, the only time I can do it is Sunday afternoon. Would that work?"

Touched by the other mom's kindness, Kelly smiled. "It'd be great, actually."

"I'm hoping we can get something regular going, so that Shoshanna feels more at home in Laramie. I'm afraid I've been so busy getting acclimated at my job, I haven't worked hard enough to provide her with a social group of her own. I want to fix that."

"I'd be glad to help."

"I also wanted to ask—one single mom to another—what you were planning to do about this." Sharon reached into her purse and pulled out an invitation.

Kelly stared down at the boldly lettered announcement. For once, completely at a loss.

Hours later, she was still ruminating over the turn of events when school concluded for the day, and she took her children out to the empty playground for their daily ritual of twenty minutes of free play before heading home.

No sooner had the triplets climbed up on the jungle gym than a shadow fell over Kelly. She turned to see Dan, looking handsome as ever in his tan uniform.

He held her gaze. She swallowed over the sudden dry feeling in her throat. "The administrator's office is—"

"That way. I know." He strode closer, and she could feel the heat emanating from his tall, muscular body.

"I already filled out the field trip papers, releasing the school from all claims of liability."

She edged away from the woodsy scent of his cologne, wishing she weren't quite so aware of him. Aching to feel his mouth on hers again. "That's good. Thank you."

Taking her by the hand, he led her toward the nearby teacher's bench. "So what's wrong?"

Kelly's heart skittered in her chest. "What do you mean?" Could he really read her mood that easily? Apparently so.

"Just now, you looked like you had lost your best friend."

Kelly sat, tugging her pretty summer skirt down to her knees. "I don't really have a best friend here yet." Although she could see Dan filling that role. And what did *that* say?

He nodded. "Me, either. Lots of casual buddies. No one special." He sat down beside her on the bench, and briefly covered her hand with his larger one. "So what's turning that smile of yours upside down?"

Feeling a little embarrassed, Kelly let out a mirthless

laugh and shook her head. The whole thing was just so humiliating. "It's a long boring story."

He puffed out his chest comically. "What do you know! My favorite kind!"

As much as she suddenly loathed to lean on his broad shoulders, she took a moment to wave at her kids before turning back to him. "I can't talk about it here."

Interest lit his mesmerizing blue eyes. "Where can you discuss it?"

"Home, I guess."

His gaze drifted over her before returning ever so slowly to her face. "Why, Ms. Kelly, are you inviting me to dinner?"

His shameless flirting brought a smile to her face. And a telltale heat welling up inside her. "I'm not sure a grown man would call it that. We're having very kid-friendly, semi-homemade fare."

"Well, what do you know?" He passed yet another of her tests with flying colors. "Also my favorite kind."

Once again, their gazes collided.

Kelly bit her lip. She did need to unburden herself, and knowing Dan, he would not let her wallow in self-inflicted misery. Decision made, she rose, signaling the kids to come to her. "As long as you understand, it's not a date."

"Not even close." He regarded her, deadpan.

She rolled her eyes. "I'm not kidding here, Deputy."

Believe me." He mocked her exaggerated tone. "I know…"

As Kelly expected, her kids were wildly excited to discover that Deputy Dan was going to have dinner with them for the second night in a row. They completely monopolized his attention and he basked in the adoring attention, while Kelly quickly whipped up supper.

Freshly cooked spaghetti, with marina sauce from a jar, and homemade chicken meatballs she pulled from the freezer and reheated. Salad for the adults. Carrot sticks with ranch dressing for the kids. And the children's favorite crescent rolls out of a tube, baked to golden brown perfection.

"Wow," Dan said as they all sat down together.

He gave her a look that said he'd been expecting a whole lot less.

Michelle added, "Mommy learned on TV. The cooking channels are her favorites!"

Dan's grin took in the whole family. "Is that so?"

Matthew added, "We watch cooking shows together!"

"Sometimes we help Mommy, too," Michael said soberly, "but *not* on school nights. She's too tired to supe'vise us then."

"Understandable," Dan said, melding into her family as easily as if he were her children's daddy.

And on it went. Nonstop chatter all through the meal. Sensing—correctly—she could use some help winding them down, Dan stayed through bath and bedtime, reading stories, bringing the excitement level down until finally Kelly was able to put them to bed.

She came downstairs to find him doing the dishes. Impossible, how masculine he looked, no matter what he was doing. She joined him by the kitchen sink. "You don't have to do this."

He set the last dish in the dishwasher, then began wiping down the counters with spray cleaner and paper towels. "My mother would say otherwise. Dinner was great, by the way."

Kelly took care of the marina sauce splatters on the stove. "The company or the food?" She shot him a look over her shoulder and found him checking out her derriere.

"Both." He flashed a mischievous grin. Clearly liking what he saw. Oh boy. They were headed for dangerous territory here.

Sobering, he took her hand and led her to the sofa. He settled next to her. Grinning when she stifled a yawn. "So, before you fall asleep, too, what was going on today that had you so upset?"

Confession time.

"I'll show you." Kelly pulled a folded piece of paper from her pocket and waved it in front of him. "This invitation went out in a mass email to all the parents at the school, but somehow did not manage to reach me, too."

Together they read the announcement, which said:

You are invited to come and help us celebrate Father's Day at the Laramie Preschool's Summer Picnic! Complete with a complimentary photo booth for Father and Family Portraits, Sack Races for Daddy and His Little Darlings, a complimentary video booth for My Favorite Memories of My Daddy, a Sing-along with Daddy, and Daddy's Favorite Treasure Hunt.

Staring at it, Dan snorted in disbelief. "A little over the top with the theme, don't you think?"

Thank you! Kelly sighed. "As you can see, it's great for kids who have a dad who can come. Not so great for those who don't."

He swiveled to face her, frowning. "Is it always this way?"

At last she wasn't the only one upset. "Apparently, although not to this in-your-face level."

"Does the school do the same thing on Mother's Day?"

Kelly sighed. "Unfortunately, yes. They hold a Mother

Daughter Tea Party that's hell for kids who either don't have a mom, or have one, but she's working and can't get time off, or in the military and deployed overseas…"

He slung his arm along the back of the sofa and pulled her into the curve of his body. "What did those kids do?"

Kelly propped her legs on the coffee table and settled against him. "Some didn't show up at all. Left town and skipped the event. Others came with a family friend, or their dad. Which, given all the frou-frou elements of the tea, was a little strange."

He propped his feet up, too. "Can't something be done about it?"

"I tried." Kelly liked the way he felt, snuggled against her. "I talked to our director about making both events less painful to those not in a two-parent home. But," she said, sighing, briefly closing her eyes as she breathed in his clean, masculine scent, "Mirabelle Evans, the mom in charge of the school's Parent League, is adamant on keeping tradition alive, as she likes to say. And because her family has donated a ton of money to the school over the years, the director does not want to cross her."

Dan rubbed his palm over her knuckles. "Are you worried about the triplets, how they are going to respond to this?"

Damn, he was perceptive. Kelly nodded. "And Shoshanna, and all the others affected."

He brought her arm up, and for a moment she thought he was going to kiss the inside of her wrist, but then he dropped it back down to her side. A surprising jolt of disappointment went through her. "What are you going to do?"

"Not sure, but I've got another week to figure it out."

He paused, serious now. "You know. I could step in for you and your kids. Tag along, as a family friend."

This was all getting dangerously tempting. Kelly warned, "People might talk…"

He shrugged, watching as she rose and walked back into the kitchen. "They talk about me, anyway."

But not me.

He followed her over to the oven. Watched as she pretended to make sure it was switched off.

He lounged in the portal, big, muscular arms folded in front of him. "Seriously," he said, giving her what was almost way too much breathing room, "if I could make things better for the triplets, I'd really like to do so."

It was for her kids.

Not her, she reminded herself in relief.

Kelly knew the excitement of having Deputy Dan at the event would prove a powerful distraction, even if he weren't in uniform, the way he had been when he had visited the preschool.

"Thank you," she said softly. "I think I'll take you up on your kind offer." *Even while keeping my heart tightly under wraps.*

He smiled.

"But there are still a lot of other kids—like Shoshanna—who won't have anyone," she worried aloud, as she got the makings of tomorrow's school lunches out of the fridge.

Dan's gaze narrowed thoughtfully. He sat on a stool on the other side of the island. "You could create a buddy system."

How was it possible the two of them could think so alike? Kelly lined up the pieces of bread. "I've been thinking about it."

Dan watched her spread peanut butter on one slice, jelly on the other, as if she were the most interesting woman in all the world. "Maybe if there were other activities, too, that weren't aimed strictly at daddy and child…"

Brainstorming with him was almost as much fun as kissing him. Kelly pushed the disturbing image away. They were not going to kiss again. Were they...? She swallowed around the sudden parched feeling in her throat, her heart beating wildly. "As in...?"

Casually, he offered, "There's a Go Fishing game and a Pin the Tail on the Donkey board that we use at the annual Laramie County Chili Festival to raise funds for the sheriff's department. They just sit in storage all year, so I'm pretty sure I could borrow them. We could also put together a beanbag toss. Maybe have a piñata that all the kids could take a swing at."

"Love it. Could we start pulling things together on Saturday, after we apologize for the goat eating the tomatoes incident to your neighbor?"

Regret tautened the handsome planes of his face. "I wish." He rose, as if getting ready to leave. "I'm working from noon to midnight. But I could bring them over on Sunday afternoon."

When the kids would be at their playdate.

Not about to quibble over timing, just so she wouldn't find herself alone with him, Kelly smiled. It would be a simple drop-off of items. Then she'd send him on his way. There'd be no more intimate chit chat or sinfully sexy looks. No casual touching or tempting kisses or anything else that might lead them astray. She nodded, bolstering her resolve. "That sounds great."

Her heart fluttering wildly in her chest, she walked him to the door. Filled with regret to find their time together ending. She turned to him. He moved in. The next thing she knew his arms were wrapped around her. They were chest to chest and thigh to thigh. She lifted her head. His mouth came down. The world narrowed to just the two of them and this moment in time. His lips were hot and sensual, tempting and caressing. Her arms curled around his shoulders and she sagged against him in equal parts surrender and wonder. She moaned, her lips parting as she reveled in the captivating pressure and tenderness of his kiss. The erotic sweep of his tongue. The feel of his heartbeat thudding quickly, in conjunction with hers.

He made her feel all woman to his man.

He made her feel as if she could be his.

And he could be hers.

That there could be an end to the loneliness she'd felt almost all her life.

Maybe even a happiness unlike anything she had ever dreamed existed.

And that was, of course, when the sinfully hot caress ended. He lifted his head and looked deep into her eyes. Content as she was flustered.

Satisfaction that went soul-deep radiated between them. "Sweet dreams," he murmured, reaching out to smooth a strand of her hair, before letting her go reluctantly.

Her lips still tingling, Kelly struggled for composure. "To you, too," she replied inanely. Knowing, after that hot clinch, they couldn't be anything but wonderful, for either of them!

Chapter Seven

"Thanks for doing this with me," Kelly told Dan when she arrived at the Bowie Creek Ranch on Saturday morning to pick him up. She wanted her kids to grow up to be responsible. Taking ownership of their mistakes from an early age was part of that.

"No problem," he said, loading the gardening supplies he'd already bought into the cargo area of her SUV. "I'm happy for the company."

She was happy, too.

Maybe more so than she should be, given the fact that she was not going to be able to lean on this big handsome man anywhere near as much as the romantic feminine part of her would like to. Even if he did kiss her and make her feel as if the two of them were meant to be...

Luckily, her kids took up all of Dan's attention as she drove to his neighbor's ranch house and parked in front of it. So all she had to do was keep her mind on the task at hand.

Not exactly an easy feat when he looked so good in jeans and a gray Texans T-shirt that hugged every taut muscle in his shoulders, chest and abs. With a sigh of regret, she reminded herself she had to be sensible, and pushed her renewed longing aside.

Oblivious to the conflicted feelings roiling around

inside her, he settled a straw hat on his head, and asked, "Everybody ready to do this?"

"Yes!" the kids said in unison. They unbuckled their safety belts and piled out of the vehicle. Like Kelly, they were wearing old clothes suitable for gardening, rubber boots and canvas sun hats.

"Is she going to be mad at us?" Michelle asked worriedly.

Good question, Kelly thought. Dan looked over at Mrs. Weller's thriving vegetable garden, which still had a large chunk chewed out of its center. He made a regretful face. "I think she's calmed down a lot, but even if she hadn't, we still have to do what we can to make amends."

Michael tugged on Dan's hand. "What's 'mends?"

"Make things right," he explained gently.

Trying not to swoon over how kind and patient Dan was with her triplets, Kelly handed each of her children a potted tomato seedling, ready for planting. Dan picked up a flat of a dozen more, and she grabbed the basket of beautiful fresh tomatoes.

All five headed for the door of the ranch house.

Mrs. Weller—who had been told to expect them—stepped out. The petite older woman was trim and fit and had short, curly white hair. She wore an apron over her flower-print blouse and jeans. Dan paused to make introductions, which were gracefully received.

"I know we can't completely make up for the loss of your crop of beautiful homegrown summer tomatoes, but we brought a new set of plants that can go in the ground now, and will produce more tomatoes for you in sixty to ninety days. Meantime, I will go to Rose Mc-Culloch's organic wholesale business every week, pick out the best of what she has, just as we have today, and bring them by."

Mrs. Weller accepted the bounty from Kelly. "Thank you. I appreciate this."

"It's the least we can do, given what happened," Dan said. "I should have kept a better eye on my goats."

Ruefully, Kelly interjected, "And I should have kept a better eye on my children, who opened the gate, allowing the goats to run away."

She turned to her children, prompting with a raised brow. "We're sorry the goats ate your garden, too," they chimed in unison.

"So, if it's okay," Dan continued, "we'd like to follow whatever instructions you have for us and do the planting for you."

Mrs. Weller smiled. She exchanged her apron for a sun hat and a pair of green rubber boots. "Let's all work together. Shall we?"

Half an hour later, the restoration was finished and they were all gathered on her front porch for freshly baked cookies and lemonade. The shortage of outdoor furniture had Mrs. Weller in the lone armchair, all three kids sitting on the chain hung swing, and Dan and Kelly sitting, thigh to thigh, in the small wicker settee.

"How's the search for a new home going?" Mrs. Weller asked Dan pointedly. "Have you found anyone who wants your goats?"

He lifted his lemonade to his lips, his shoulder bumping Kelly's in the process. "I put up a sign in the feed store a month ago. But since they're pets, and not bred to produce either meat or dairy, I haven't gotten any takers."

The kids regarded him quizzically.

Kelly turned to Dan, her glance warning him not to explain the different uses for an animal they viewed strictly as a pet. Happily, he got it and said nothing more on the topic. Unfortunately, her brief swivel had pushed the curve of her breast against his sinewy bicep. Heat pooled through her, and her nipples were still tingling when she turned away. She tried shifting unobtrusively sideways, to put a little space between them, but the only thing that happened was she slid even closer to the middle of the settee, and hence, him.

Oblivious to the havoc being squished up against Dan was having on Kelly, Mrs. Weller pulled a small square of card stock from her pocket. "I may have a solution for you, Dan." She leaned forward to hand it to him.

"I spoke with Orin Franklin, a west Texas farmer and businessman and told him what only two of your runaways did to my vegetable patch. He's definitely interested in acquiring them."

Dan's expression was inscrutable. "Thanks."

Concerned how her kids might react to the notion of the goats being sold, Kelly slanted a glance at them. To her relief, the discussion thus far, was completely over their heads.

Dan seemed equally on alert, even as Mrs. Weller persisted. "Because you're definitely going to have to do something soon. Isn't this the third time they've run away?"

He drained his glass and set it on the floor. In an obvious move to give them more room, Dan sat back and draped his arm along the back of the settee.

Kelly was able to lean forward slightly, so they weren't touching from the waist up. Lower, well, they were still hip to hip and thigh to thigh. Able to feel each other's damp heat emanating through their clothing.

Dan nodded affably at their hostess. He continued talking about the pets he'd inadvertently acquired with the purchase of his home. "You're right. They've all gotten out at one time or another since I moved in two months ago. But to be perfectly honest, most of that was my fault. I hadn't built an adequately high enclosure. Or taken proper precautions by putting a lock on the gate. Now I have."

"You're telling me you really want to put in the time and attention it takes to properly care for a pet goat, never mind an entire herd of them?"

Dan had no immediate answer for that.

"They'll be happier elsewhere," Mrs. Weller insisted. She rose regally. "So the sooner you move them to a new home, the better."

"MOMMY, HOW COME the goats are going to a new home?" Michael asked when they were driving away again. Regretting the fact her kids had finally realized what was being discussed, Kelly maneuvered the short distance to Dan's ranch and turned into the long lane.

"Are the goats moving?" Matthew wanted to know.

Michelle's voice trembled. "I don't like moving."

Michael added, "Won't they be scared if they have to live somewhere else?"

Not sure how to answer that, since she didn't know what was going to happen next, either, Kelly turned to Dan.

As gently as if he were their daddy, he said, "First, I'm not going to do anything that is going to make the goats unhappy."

He turned to Kelly and reached across the console to briefly squeeze her forearm. She slanted him a glance. The look in his eyes clearly said *I'm not going to do anything to make any of you unhappy.*

She drew a quick breath.

"Second, Mrs. Weller was right. I may not be the best owner for the goats. I work long hours at my job. Although I muck out their pen, and make sure they have plenty of food and water, I don't have time to play with them the way their previous owners did."

"We could play with them for you!" Michelle insisted.

"Yeah!" her brothers chimed in. "That way they'd have friends."

"We could even play with them today!" Michael surprised Kelly by volunteering.

Not waiting to see if Dan was amenable to that idea or not, Kelly looked at her watch and gave them both an out. "Actually, kids, Dan has to go to work, and since it's Saturday, we have things to do today, too. Laundry and grocery shopping, and going to the gas station to put gas in Mommy's SUV and run it through the car wash, too."

The kids groaned.

"And we'll be back with all your classmates during the field trip on Monday."

"That's not the same, Mommy," Michelle pouted.

Kelly understood. Venturing out to Bowie Creek ranch with nearly one hundred others did not begin to compare with the intimacy of the other evening, when they'd visited with the goats, learned how to clean their boots, enjoyed a light supper, and chased fireflies on the lawn. The womanly side of her longed to spend more time with him, too. Both with her kids and without. Heck, if she were honest, she'd admit she wished they could get in a few more stolen kisses. Which—given her determination not to get any more emotionally involved with him than she already had—wasn't good.

Luckily, the only time they technically had to see each other again in an intimate setting, at least in the near future, would be when he delivered the games she was borrowing from him for the summer picnic.

She could handle that, especially if the kids weren't around to cheerlead on his behalf.

Couldn't she?

"IT'S AWFULLY QUIET around here," Dan remarked on Sunday afternoon when he arrived with the promised games. Kelly smiled, trying not to reveal how her pulse was racing. "The triplets are at a playdate with Shoshonna at Sharon's house." It was also the first time since the last time they'd kissed that the two of them were completely without chaperones.

She'd armed herself against intimacy with activity, with two-foot squares of medium sailcloth spread over her wraparound front porch. Circular targets had been drawn on each, and would soon be painted on for better visibility.

He ambled closer, observing the way she painted black circles on the cloth. He smelled good. Like soap and sun and man. "When do you pick them up?"

This was the first time she'd seen him in anything but a uniform or jeans. It was amazing how good he looked in a pair of knee-length charcoal gray shorts, V-necked T-shirt and serious running shoes that looked like they'd pounded out more than a few miles.

So he wasn't just country; he could be summer in the city, too.

Aware he was still awaiting an answer, she put down the paint can in her hand and said, "Five o'clock." Three hours from now. Three impossibly long, impossibly short hours.

He nodded, his thoughts about that indecipherable. "Where are you going to want the games I brought over?" he asked, inclining his head at his truck.

Together, they walked over. All too aware of him at

her side, Kelly surveyed the Go Fishing and the Pin the Tail on the Donkey carnival-style games in the bed of his pickup. They were made of solid wood, and a little bigger and bulkier than she had imagined. Too much so for her to easily move around on her own.

She pursed her lips, considering. "I was going to put them in my garage. But, seeing them—" she pivoted toward him and met his gorgeous azure blue eyes "—I think it might be better to have them in the storage room at the rear of my classroom." That way, she thought, when it came to picnic time, all they'd have to do was carry them out to the school lawn for placement.

The corners of his sensual lips curved up. He seemed to know the effect his easy masculine presence was having on her, darn it. "You want to do that this afternoon?"

She'd like to do a lot of things this afternoon…

But he was right. It would be easier to unload and store the games without teachers, parents and/or students around. "Sure." Kelly sighed.

There was only problem with that.

"You want to get your painting done first, don't you?"

Marveling at his ability to read her mind, she swept a hand through her hair—or tried to, until she realized she'd already put it up in a clip. "It's just that the targets need to dry before I put them all away, and that needs to happen before the triplets come home." Otherwise, mass chaos would definitely ensue.

He gave her a long look. "Want me to help?"

She hadn't thought so. Now that he was here, though, looking so big and strong and masculine…so determined, it was a lot harder to refuse him. "Sure you wouldn't mind?"

"Not in the least." He walked back up the steps with her and looked down at her project. "What is this, anyway?"

Kelly tried not to notice the dark hair feathering his

muscular arms and legs, peeking out of the V of his shirt, or wonder if he was that potently male all over.

Telling herself she was stepping into the shade, and not away from him, she used her ultrapleasant classroom voice to inform him, "It's a preschool version of a beanbag toss."

Aware he was now noticing what she was wearing—knit workout shorts that in retrospect showed far too much leg, a tank top she didn't care if she got paint on and flip-flops—she flushed and turned away.

Pretending the heat in her cheeks was due to the rising June temperature, and not the hunger she noted in his intrigued gaze, she continued her tour of the project-in-process. "I'm making targets that we'll lay on the grass." She lifted one to illuminate. "Each circle will be marked with a different color. The children will get six chances to toss their bags at the targets, and then we'll let them choose a toy prize from the colored bin of their choice. It won't matter if they actually land a bag on that particular color or not. We'll just have them identify the color they land on every time they make a toss."

Approval radiated in his gaze. "So it's a learning experience, and everybody wins."

She smiled. "That is the goal."

His eyes skimmed her head to toe. "Sweet."

"Thanks." Telling herself it did not matter if she impressed him or not, she handed him a brush and a small can of the black paint.

After opening up several more cans, she began painting red inside the outermost rings, as did he. "So how are your goats?"

He moved to the opposite end of the porch, which gave them each plenty of room to work. "Okay, although I had a problem this morning. One was walking like something was wrong with her feet. So I called Sara Anderson—the vet I use—and she came over. Turned out the hooves needed trimming." Dan painted with the same sure deftness he did everything else. "Sarah brought a stanchion and some shears and showed me how to do it."

"Was it difficult?"

"No, but it's something that apparently has to be done to every one of the goats every six weeks. Although the other five don't quite need it yet."

Twenty-four hooves, total. "Sounds like a lot of work," Kelly sympathized.

He nodded, for a moment looking as overwhelmed as she felt on some days with the triplets. "More than I really have time for when you consider the rest of their care. The feeding and watering and mucking out their pen."

The latter of which was not pleasant, Kelly knew. Finished with the red, she opened up a can of grass green. "Did you call the person Mrs. Weller suggested?"

He offered a curt nod. "And…?" She watched him walk down the porch to rinse the brushes with the garden hose.

"He owns a business that rents out miniature goats to clear property of scrub."

Kelly took him a stack of clean rags on which to dry them. "Sounds useful."

Another nod.

Their hands rubbed against each other as they worked on the chore together. "But something bothers you."

Dan exhaled.

Together, they remounted the steps. "Orin Franklin doesn't have a system for containing the goats while they work. He just drops them off and goes back later, when the land is cleared, and picks them up."

"So in the meantime…" Kelly guessed, horrified.

His lips compressed. "Anything could happen. They could wander off. Get lost. End up on the highway and get hit by a car."

Something that, as a lawman who worked the county roads, Dan had probably dealt with.

Kelly paused. "Is that why he needs more goats?"

Dan winced and went back to painting. "Apparently business is booming, but he's had some unexpected casualties."

The image was devastating. Kelly knelt, too. "Oh, dear," she said, picking up her brush. "I can't see me telling the triplets that the goats are off to do that!"

"Me, either." Dan's arm and shoulders flexed as he painted with long, powerful strokes. "So I told the guy thanks but no thanks. I'll keep looking for another solution."

"Hopefully," Kelly said with a sigh, shaking her head, "it will be one the kids can understand and accept."

He paused to look over at her, all indomitable male again. Kelly blushed. She couldn't blame him for being surprised. She was talking like their lives would continue to be entwined!

"I mean, not that this is your problem," she added hastily, slipping back inside the house to get more craft brushes so they wouldn't have to rinse and dry every time they switched colors. She emerged from the house and handed his over. "I just don't want them worried about this."

Dan sat back on his haunches. His brows knit together. "They're still upset about the goats leaving my ranch?"

"Very much so," Kelly admitted reluctantly.

They'd both finished the green so were now on to the purple. "Why?" he asked in concern.

Wondering if she had ever met a man who was so

compassionate and intuitive, Kelly said, "They can't visualize the unknown. And they don't like moving in general."

"Even to Laramie?"

Kelly appreciated being able to talk so candidly with the handsome lawman. "Change is hard for anyone, Dan, and for kids it's even more so since the familiar equals security."

Done with the green, they moved on to the yellow.

He regarded her intently. "You're talking about personal experience now?"

Kelly nodded. "I didn't realize how attached they were to the townhome in Dallas. For me, it was just a temporary rental while I figured out my next steps. But to them it was the only home they had ever known."

"So moving here…?"

"…into this house was initially pretty traumatic for them." Aware they'd gotten too close, Kelly stopped painting. Waiting, watching him, until she could resume.

"Fortunately," she said, moving sideways, "I had to start working practically right away, and they were at the preschool with me, so." She smiled, recalling, "That proved both a nice introduction to the community and a distraction."

Aware they had two colors to go, Dan opened up the can of orange. Kelly took over the blue.

They painted, the silence almost as comforting as the conversation. "So how did you end up here?" Dan asked eventually.

Kelly gathered up all the used brushes and took them down to the grass. She laid them out, side by side, and began to hose them off.

"It was one of those things that felt like it was fated."

He took over for her. "How so?"

"I was looking to get out of the city, into a more idyllic environment, and go back to work."

They dried off the brushes, and then she led the way inside the house. "I met Cece Taylor, one of my colleagues, at a continuing education workshop." She went straight for the kitchen. "She told me how great Laramie was, and that there was an opening at her school that hadn't been filled." Taking two bottles of chilled water out of the fridge, she tossed him one. They both took long thirsty drinks. "I applied and I got it."

"I'm not surprised," he drawled, lounging against the counter opposite her.

She lifted a questioning brow.

"From what I saw the day I was a guest speaker in your class, you are a very good teacher."

His praise warmed her through and through. "Thanks."

She paused, realizing they were both a little sweaty, and that on him, anyway, the damp clothing looked very good. She let her gaze drift over him. Aware there was still much she wanted to know about him, as well. "Why did *you* come back to Laramie to live after working elsewhere?"

Their eyes locking; he stepped forward. The next thing she knew he had a hand clamped on either side of her. "Because I felt like I'd find the woman I was meant to be with here," he rasped.

He leaned in, lowering his head. "And, what do you know," he murmured, his smile pressed against her lips, "I have…"

Kelly hadn't expected him to kiss her. But now that he was, she wasn't about to let him stop.

She needed him to do this. Needed to know there

was either something really special between them, or there wasn't.

Needed to be able to get the urge to make love with him—hot, wild tempestuous love—out of her system, so she could go back to the reality of her everyday life, and stop wanting the impossible, a once in a lifetime love, with him.

Because that wasn't going to happen.

Not with someone as wonderful and sought after as him.

Dan was destined to be with someone who had shared the kind of exemplary childhood he had, and hence was likely to be accepted by his wealthy family in a way she never could be. Someone who not only trusted in the vagaries of romantic love, but knew how to give it in the deep abiding way he no doubt expected.

Not with a woman who'd grown up in chaos, and had been in and out of foster care.

Needing the comfort she found with him even more, she fisted her hands in his shirt and held him close, the heat of her body mingling pleasurably with his. He moaned even as her body shivered in anticipation.

"Kelly..."

"I know." She let her tongue play with his, fighting and losing the battle with the desire that had been plaguing her since they'd first met. "Bad idea..."

"Really bad idea." Eyes turbulent, he swept his hands down to cup her hips.

Trouble was, it felt so good. *He* felt so good.

She went up on tiptoe, giving in to temptation and better molding her curves to his hard, muscular planes. Her hands slid beneath his shirt, even as her lips discovered the U of his collarbone. Yearning washed over her. The two previous times he'd kissed her, he'd made her feel sexy, vibrant, alive. She wanted that feeling again, wanted to know that, even for a short while, it was okay, when she was with him, to let down her guard.

That he wouldn't hurt her.

Would only savor her.

Savor *this*.

And boy, she thought, as they came together ardently again, were their kisses and caresses worth savoring. Their tongues tangled and their lips melded, as he kissed her again and again, as if he meant to have her and make her his. She loved the way he tasted, the way he seemed to drink her in, even as he encouraged to come out to play the way she hadn't in, well, ever. Hungry for more of him, she pressed even closer, molding her body to his. Wanting to feel connected to him, not just body to body, but heart and soul.

Eventually, he stopped again, just long enough to reluctantly rein in his intense male energy. Cup her head in his big hands and moan, "We don't have to do this."

Because of course, he was, at heart, a gentleman, and gentlemen didn't take advantage of women who wouldn't even date them.

Except, she thought, as she felt the pulsing heat of his lower body, he wasn't taking advantage. She was.

She arched against him in abject surrender. Letting him know that with a wink and a smile, "I think we do…" She kicked off her flip-flops, took him by the hand and led him toward the stairs.

They hit the second floor. He took her in with eyes gone dark, intense. "Because…?"

She turned, leaning up against the wall, aware it had been a long time since she'd felt this beautiful and desirable, but whenever he looked at her, she did. She wanted to hang on to that. Hang on to him…at least for the here and now. "So we'll know," she returned softly, the prom-

ise in her low voice matching his, "what heaven is…"
And then could come to their senses, and move on…

Dan knew what was going on here.

Kelly wanted to rush into something so she'd feel jus-
tified in calling it quits before they even had a chance. He
knew she thought she'd regret this, and maybe she would,
in the short term. In the long run, he hoped she'd see it
as the beginning of something fantastic. He knew he did.

Body aching with need, he guided her against him.
Moving his palm over her spine until her soft breasts
nestled against his chest. She swayed slightly, her knees
wobbling. Her mouth softened against his, opening to
allow him greater access. And just that swiftly they were
back on the path to fulfillment. Need poured out of her,
matching his own. Succumbing to the moment, too, he
pulled her in, enjoying the adrenaline rush of their reckless tryst.

Still kissing, she led him toward her bed. They tum-
bled onto it. Unwrapped each other simultaneously, then
paused to enjoy the sexy sight. "Damn, Kelly, you're
beautiful."

She grinned in admiration. "So are you…"

Libido roaring, body hard, he ran his hands over her
breasts, her taut pink nipples, the silky insides of her
thighs. She caught her breath, her back arched. Then he
was rising above her. Guiding her against him, giving her
a long thorough kiss designed to seduce her into further
lowering the barriers around her heart. She was wild in a
way he could never have imagined, as giving as he could
have wished. Then he was moving back down, slowly and
persuasively. Stopping to kiss and caress every pleasure
point along the way. She caressed him in turn until her
cry of ecstasy had him grinning in masculine satisfaction. "Now," she whispered.

"Now," he promised gruffly. He found the condom, rolled it on. And then they were kissing again, her mouth molding to the plundering pressure of his. Lower still, she was wet and open. He was hot and hard. Amazing, he thought, as he finally made her his, how well, how perfectly they fit. Like she was made for him, and he for her.

Emotions soaring, he lifted her, going deeper, slower, stronger. As eager for completion as he, she received him with the same single-minded intensity. And then there was nothing but the rise to fulfillment and the sweet, hot melting bliss.

DAN FELT KELLY'S regret as strongly as he had felt her passion just moments before. Cheeks flooded with color, she rose.

Taking his cue from her, he reluctantly began to dress, too. It wasn't as if he hadn't known this was coming given the fact she was the least impulsive woman he had ever met.

Her back to him, she said, "You know, I've changed my mind about taking the games over to the preschool. We're not going to have time for that."

She was probably right since she'd said she had to pick her triplets from their playdate at five o'clock.

Kelly ran a brush through her hair. "I think I'll just store them here, in my garage, and take them over on the day of the summer picnic. Or if you prefer, you can keep them at your place."

"How about I keep them in my barn?" he suggested, figuring he could at least be gallant about this. It would also be an excuse to see each other. And he had the feeling that after this he would need a lot of excuses if he wanted to see her. "Then you won't have to worry about lugging them around."

She slipped into the bathroom to repair her makeup. "Sounds good."

When she came back out, they stared at each other awkwardly. "Well," she said, focusing all her attention on her wristwatch, "thanks again."

"For making love to you?"

Self-conscious color stained her sculpted cheeks. "For helping with the target painting."

He moved closer not about to pretend, even if she was. "You know, Kelly, what happened between us is a good thing." It hurt, to see her acting as if it weren't.

Her breath hitched. "No," she said, still looking up at a point past his shoulder. "It's not. It was reckless."

"And you're not reckless."

This time she did look him in the eye. "I've got three kids who rely solely on me, Dan. So, no." Her lower lip trembled. "I'm not. Usually, anyway."

He was willing to bet it was more like not ever. Until he had come along, and persuaded her otherwise. Guilt flooded through him. He knew how vulnerable she was, that he shouldn't have rushed things. But they had, so they were going to have to deal with it. And doing so meant speaking honestly. "I'm not reckless either, Kelly." He wasn't sure she believed him. He pushed on softly, "And if you'll give me a chance, I'll prove it to you."

Her eyes widened. "You mean, see you again?"

He told himself Kelly hadn't just been using him, to discover the truth about Shoshanna. The way Belinda had used him to discover what was going on in regard to her father.

"As on another date with just the two of us," he bartered, "yes."

A wary look from beneath her lashes. She glided away from him. Propping both her hands on her luscious hips, pivoted and said, "I don't think I can do that, Dan." Her voice trembled slightly. "I don't think it would be wise."

Telling himself his life was not about to take a sharp downward turn again, the way it had before, he studied her silently. Then countered, just as softly, "And if I do…?"

Sadness came and went in her eyes. Followed by a hint of longing. "Still, no." The defiant edge was back in her voice.

He knew what she wanted him to believe. That their lovemaking had been a physical release for her, nothing more. There was only one problem with that. Kelly wasn't the type of woman who would allow herself to be that vulnerable, if her heart wasn't somehow involved.

Realizing it was going to take time and persistence, to convince her that he would never hurt her the way the triplets' father had, he closed the distance between them, wrapped his arms around her, and said, "I'm not giving up, Kelly."

She splayed her hands across his chest. Her eyes took on a turbulent sheen. "You should."

"And you want to know why?" he prodded, lifting her chin to his.

She let out a quavering laugh. "I have a feeling you're about to tell me."

Sensing a chink in her armor, he lowered his head to deliver one last, lingering heartfelt kiss. "Because," he continued gruffly, "what happened between us just now… meant…everything to me."

And if his instincts were correct? To her, too.

Chapter Eight

"Me time really agrees with you," Sharon noted, a short while later as she greeted Kelly upon arrival.

Still a little shaken by Dan's romantic declaration regarding what had been supposed to be—in her view anyway—a no-strings encounter, Kelly moved through the doorway of Sharon's bungalow. Although it was steamy hot outside, it was nice and cool inside. "What do you mean?" Once again, she had to pretend she wasn't completely thrilled by Dan McCabe's romantic pursuit of her. Or the sense that no matter how hard she tried, she would not be able to resist him for long.

Sharon smiled. "Your skin is positively glowing."

In the aftermath of making love with Dan, Kelly felt like every single inch of her was glowing, from the inside out. Not about to discuss why, though, she admired Sharon's pink yoga capris, layered white and pink tank tops, and matching ballet flats, complimenting her. "And you're looking awfully fit." As well as overheated.

Kelly glanced at all four kids, who were gathered at the breakfast-room table, working diligently on some sort of art project. She turned back to the other mom, wondering at her flushed state. "Have you been working out again?"

Sharon sighed and shook her head. "Just weekend

chores. Sunday is my only day to get anything done around the house."

Kelly commiserated. "I know what you mean."

At Sharon's invitation, she set down her bag and took a seat in one of the wing chairs in the cozy living room. "How have the kids been? Good, I hope?"

"They were wonderful." Sharon sat down, too. "Shoshanna is so much happier, now that she's making friends. By the way, I got your note about the school's, um—" she cast a cautious look at the fatherless kids, then chose the rest of her words carefully "—*mid-June* picnic." As their eyes met, single mom to single mom, her demeanor relaxed. "I like your idea. I'm in."

Kelly lifted a cautioning hand. "I still have to speak with the administrator and the organizers of the event."

Sharon sighed. "Mirabelle Evans…"

"And a few others." Although Mirabelle's cooperation was the one they needed most. "But I wanted to find out if other parents were interested first."

Sharon put a hand to her abruptly perspiring forehead. A deep pink flush moved from her chest into her neck and face. "And are they?"

"Everyone who has responded to my email so far has been a yes." Kelly paused as Sharon grew even redder. Concerned, she couldn't help but ask, "Are you okay?"

"It's just a hot flash." Looking embarrassed, Sharon rose and went to the fridge. She pulled out a couple of bottles of chilled water, and an ice pack to hold against her chest. "The first signs of menopause. And what you will one day find out—in what I hope is the very distant future for you—is absolutely no fun!"

Kelly accepted the beverage with a nod of thanks, sympathizing. She estimated she had another twenty years before she hit the change of life. Time in which, if she wanted, she could fall in love, marry and expand her family. An idea that before that very afternoon, and the intimate interlude with Dan, had never materialized. But it was there now. Partly because he was so determined to get married and have a family himself. And partly because he was the kind of strong, gentle and loving man she had always wanted should she ever dare to marry again. The problem was, with her tumultuous childhood and embarrassing first marriage, she wasn't everything he needed—or his family would likely want—in his wife.

And she had learned the hard way that relationships did not work without the blessing of family.

Which meant, unhappily, that anything long term— anything she and her kids could depend upon—was not going to be achievable.

It was possible, of course, that she and Dan could sustain a platonic relationship, if they could somehow put the sizzling attraction between them aside. Having Dan in her life in a casual sense was better than not having him at all. So, for all their sakes, she would just have to figure out a way to steer the two of them back into the Just Friends zone.

THE REST OF Kelly's day flew by. Monday morning was even more hectic. "You look frazzled," Dan remarked as Kelly got off the preschool bus, ahead of the other chaperones and students.

Admiring how masculine he looked in the white Western shirt, and jeans, boots, a straw hat drawn low across his brow, she walked toward him. "What can I say?" she quipped, wishing she'd thought to bring a hat to shield herself from the heat, too. "We've had a crazy busy start to the morning."

One that had been almost as unexpected as their fierce and passionate lovemaking the afternoon before.

Dan stood shoulder to shoulder with her, while they waited for the second bus to make its way down the lane. He slanted her a comforting glance.

He stood, legs braced apart, arms folded in front of him. "In what way?"

Reminding herself she had decided to be sensible. They were going to be just friends now. Kelly resisted the urge to throw herself into his arms for a brief hug and kiss hello.

Something that wasn't easy to do given the fact that Dan looked like he were privately tempted to do the same.

Her heart skittering in her chest, Kelly returned her attention to the approaching school bus. And explained, "Shoshanna showed up for the field trip wearing the wrong clothes. I caught Sharon as she was driving away, and she was a mess. Apparently what she thought were hot flashes yesterday was actually the beginning of a virus of some sort. She was up all night with fever and stomach woes, and planning to take more acetaminophen and anti-nausea meds and go back to bed as soon as she got Shoshanna off to preschool. So, it's no wonder she forgot about the rule that all students must be wearing their bright orange Laramie Preschool summer T-shirt, long pants and closed toe shoes on any outdoor field trips." Where there could potentially be biting insects and poison ivy, and all manner of things.

Dan's gaze drifted over her, much as it had the day they'd made love. When he caught her noticing, the corners of his sensual lips turned up.

Shoulders taut, body braced for action, eyes gleaming appreciably. He worked to maintain appearances and kept up the easy conversation. "It's completely understandable that she would forget," he said in his low gravelly voice that sent shivers up Kelly's spine. "Especially since Sharon and Shoshanna are still relatively new to the school and the area." Once again, Kelly noted with pleasure, Dan seemed to inherently understand how difficult being a single parent could sometimes be.

Flashing him a grateful smile, Kelly continued, "Anyway, I slow-walked the check-in process for the field trip while Sharon rushed her little girl back home and got her changed, and then back to school just in time to board the bus with the other kids."

Dan's expression sobered. He stepped nearer, compassion radiating. "Are you going to help her out later?"

"I offered." Kelly pushed aside the niggling suspicion that something more might be amiss. "But Sharon already has her regular sitter coming to pick Shoshanna up from school, as usual, and Mrs. Durant will be there to help out this evening. Staying the night, if need be, although Sharon does not think that will be necessary. She thinks it's just a twenty-four-hour bug."

The second bus came up the lane.

One of the four-year-old-class teachers got off bus two, along with several parent chaperones.

Kelly turned to Dan. "Ready to do this?" she asked, her heart thrilling all over again at his proximity. It was going to be harder than she thought to stay in the friends zone.

He nodded, his expression intent. "I am."

Kelly and the other teachers helped the students off the buses. In orderly procession, they headed for the tall goat pen Dan had built.

It looked like he had bathed the miniature pet goats before the students arrived. They were snowy white, with splotches of silky ebony here and there.

He had definitely mucked out the pen. And put little collars on all six.

One by one, he snapped on a lead and brought them out to meet the students.

After each introduction was made, a name was plucked out of the bowl they'd brought with them.

And the official naming commenced.

By the time they were done, they had Katie, Penny, Daisy, Becky, Sherrie and Sally.

"I'm sensing a theme here," Dan said, as the goats were returned to the pen and students sat in the shade of some nearby trees, eating Popsicles.

Because some of the students had a fear of dogs, Shep had been kept in his crate inside the house.

Kelly kept her eyes on the students they were chaperoning. She knit her brow in amusement. "For some reason, when we were adding names to the bowls, almost all of them ended with the *e* sound."

Dan squinted. "There's a definite symmetry to it."

She chuckled. "Now *you* sound like a teacher…"

Without warning, Mirabelle Evans walked up. The rail-thin brunette was garbed in the obligatory bright orange school chaperone shirt, thousand-dollar jeans and a pair of equally expensive high-heeled cowgirl boots. Two-carat diamond studs glittered in her ears. Kelly imagined the necklace and tennis bracelet she wore were equally pricey.

More big-city socialite than small-town resident, she glared at both of them. "Ms. Shackleford, may I have a word with you?" The power mom stepped to the side. Kelly moved with her. She wasn't sure what this was going to be about. She only knew she dreaded it.

Mirabelle continued critically, "I've heard about what you're trying to do to ruin the preschool summer picnic."

Ruin? Kelly blinked. That was a little extreme. "Excuse me?"

"Whether you like it or not, we are using this occasion to celebrate Father's Day."

"I'm not trying to prevent that."

Mirabelle snapped, "Your actions say otherwise!"

Kelly drew a breath and tried again. "I really don't think this is the time or place—"

Mirabelle came closer. "What gave you the right to think you can alter the seating arrangements?"

"I was going to talk to you." Although she had been dreading that, too.

"And suggest four long rectangular tables, I know, I heard." She huffed out a breath. "Well, just so you know, it's not going to happen because we don't have any."

Kelly begged to differ. "The school owns four."

"And all four of them are going to be used for the buffet. The rest will be provided by my husband's Party Outfitters business, and they will all be round! So unless you can magically produce some on your own, you're out of luck! And you can tell that to everyone you've spoken to about your lamebrained idea thus far!" Mirabelle stormed off.

"Testy," Dan murmured beneath his breath.

He had no idea. Kelly felt like she had just stepped into the lion's den. She was still feeling that way hours later, as she went upstairs to wash her face and brush her teeth and get ready for bed. And that was, of course, when her cell phone chimed.

DAN KNEW IT was late when he got off work that evening, but her light was on. So he took a chance, pulled over to the curb and called her at ten thirty that evening.

Moments later, she was easing open the front door

and stepping onto the front porch in a pair of trim thigh-length workout shorts, a loose-fitting button-up, worn with the sleeves rolled up and open at the neck. Her hair was loose and looked as if it had just been thoroughly brushed. Her pretty face was as bare as her feet. And she smelled like face soap and minty toothpaste. All of which made him think she'd been in the process of getting ready for bed.

Her amber eyes, however, were as alert—and curious—as could be. She took in his uniform, as well as his own truck at the curb. "What's up?"

He shrugged, downplaying his protectiveness. "Just wanted to check on you. See how you were doing after the blowup with Mirabelle." *And maybe see if I could convince you to give me another chance and be more than friends with me.*

Momentarily looking as wary as she had after they'd made love, she turned and eased the door shut behind her. "I'm fine." She walked over to sit down on the chain hung swing, turning in the wooden seat to face him. Tilting her head to one side, she let out a tremulous sigh. "My plans to ease the hurt for the fatherless kids are in shambles, though…"

Glad she wanted to talk now the way they hadn't been able to earlier in the day, he sat down beside her. His khaki-clad thigh bumped up against her bare knee. "You can't have the additional games and distractions?"

Kelly propped her elbow on the back of the swing. She rested her head on her upturned hand, the barriers around her heart firmly in place.

He told himself that was okay, even if they were back at square one. He had coaxed her to open herself up to romance once, he could do it again.

Oblivious to his determination, she raked her teeth

across the lush ripeness of her lower lip, and said, "The preschool director said I can go ahead with that. And I even have plenty of volunteers to run the various activities."

He was beginning to see her trust issues went far beyond him. "Then…?"

She sighed and shook her head, candidly meeting his eyes. "The difficulty remains in the seating. Mirabelle is planning to do the same thing she did during the Mother's Day tea. Have assigned seats with only one family per table. For clans like hers—with their six kids and two parents—it will be a large group, and probably placed front and center. For me it won't be so bad since I'll have all three kids. But for Sharon and Shoshonna and a number of others, it will just be the two of them."

He tried not to admire the seductive strip of skin between them hem of her shorts and her knees. He lifted his gaze, taking in a brief but pleasurable glimpse of her slender waist and full breasts, before returning to her face. "Are all the tables the same size?"

"No." She let out a rough exhalation of breath. "She uses everything from a small patio table to a big one."

He reached over and gave her hand a brief squeeze. "Because she wants each group to have privacy and or individual cohesiveness? Or because she wants to demonstrate some sort of social hierarchy?" The same kind Kelly's ex-in-laws had imposed on her. In kicking her not just out of their lives, but out of the state!

Kelly shrugged and looked down at their entwined fingers. Unhappiness tautened the delicate features of her face. "Beats me. All I know is that the people at the patio tables definitely appear ill at ease."

Happy she hadn't pulled away from his attempt to comfort her physically, he tucked an errant strand of her hair behind her ear. "You can't put two or three families at one table?"

She angled her chin. "That's what I was trying to do with my rectangular tables. Create a buddy system for the families who only have one parent who can show up. On the theory that if you had several families at one table, it wouldn't be so obvious that in this case there were no fathers present for some of the kids, and/or that the men who were there were relatives or family friends, and so on."

For the first time he realized that being a single mom bothered her on some level. Just the way being only partially welcomed into her life bothered him. "But Mirabelle doesn't want that," he guessed.

Kelly stood and paced to the end of the front porch. Stood with her hands in her back pockets, looking up at the night sky.

In that moment, she looked as lonely and alone as he had often felt, after his life had fallen apart in Chicago and his heart went out to her.

Kelly pivoted partway to face him. "Obviously not. I'm sure she thinks it dilutes from the daddy theme of the picnic."

Wishing she'd open herself up to more than just friendship between them, Dan joined her where she stood. "But you'd still like to continue with your plan." *Just as I'm going to continue to do everything I can to take our relationship to the next level.*

She perched on the railing, gazing up at him, looking more inherently gorgeous than ever. "The director gave me permission to do so—if I can come up with rectangular tables and chairs to seat forty to fifty guests. Plus table linens and a seating chart for those participating in one week's time that won't in any way detract from what Mirabelle Evans already has planned."

Sounded like an impossible task. He lounged next to her. "Overwhelmed?"

Kelly wrinkled her nose. "More like defeated—at least temporarily."

He arched a brow. Waited.

She threw up a slender hand. "I don't have a vehicle to transport all those tables and chairs, never mind the budget to rent them, given that it's prime wedding season and items like that are in high demand. Especially for Saturday-evening events."

Finally. A way he could help! And an activity that just might bring them closer. "Lucky for you," he said with a grin, "I know just where you can get them."

"You're sure your mom and dad don't mind us dropping by like this?" Kelly asked early the following evening. She didn't know why. She was usually comfortable in casual social situations. But she felt a little nervous about meeting Dan's family. She slanted him a cautious glance as they walked to his pick-up truck. "Especially when they're getting ready to go out of town tomorrow?"

Dan opened the passenger door for her. "Not at all. They're always ready to help the community at large." He circled around and climbed behind the wheel. "And Mom wanted to be there to show you the various table linen options." Hand resting on the key in the ignition, he looked her over. "You're not nervous about meeting them, are you?"

Kelly settled into the worn leather seat. "It just seems a little soon," she admitted as he started the truck. Amending with a blush, "Or it would, if we were actually dating…"

He smiled, interested. "There are some who would consider this a date."

Kelly blushed and watched the scenery go by as they drove out of town. "I think it falls into the errand category."

His mouth quirked, but he held his silence.

When he said nothing more, she finally had to ask, "You don't agree?"

"Tomato, tomahta." His voice was relaxed, but it was clear he was done bartering for more.

Especially when he was getting pretty much everything he wanted anyway. Aware he was still intent on making her his, again, she made a face at him. Sighed. Wondering how long she'd be able to hold him at arm's length after all. When just being alone with him like this made her want to get to know him even more intimately, and kiss and make love to him all over again...

If only he hadn't come from such a well-connected, wealthy Texas family...but instead been from circumstances such as her own...

Kelly released another troubled sigh.

"Relax." He turned into the sprawling forty-thousand-acre cattle and horse ranch he had grown up on, with its long paved drive, plentiful outbuildings and herds of livestock. The two-story stone-and-cedar ranch house was even more impressive. Dan squeezed her shoulder. "Everyone loves my mom and dad."

Minutes later, Kelly saw why. The handsome sixty-something couple were warm and outgoing. Frank was an inch or so shy of Dan's height, but bore the same broad shoulders and taut physique. Eyes that saw...everything. Rachel was petite and blond. The perfect complement to her husband.

While the men went off to get the tables and chairs out

of storage in the room behind the garage and load them up in the ranch trailer, Rachel escorted Kelly through the comfortably decorated house.

"Please excuse the mess." She waved at the stacks of prepared handouts on the dining-room table, ready to be boxed up, and the suitcases already in the foyer.

"It's like this every year when I head to my annual tax conference. I have to organize my clothes and the materials I need for the seminars I teach." She headed up the wide staircase to the second floor. "And then there is Frank's wardrobe, too."

"You pack for him?"

"We made a deal the first year we were married to do for each other the chores we both hate the most. For him, it's anything to do with clothing and grocery shopping. He'd just as soon I take care of all that for him. He sees to my car repairs and maintenance and saddles my horse for me. So it all works out."

No wonder Dan wanted to be married, if this was what he'd grown up with. "Sounds nice."

"It is." Rachel paused to size Kelly up, in much the same way her son often did. Then led her over to a gigantic linen closet in the middle of the upstairs hall. "So, tell me more about this picnic the preschool is having."

Briefly, Kelly explained.

"What color table linens?"

"White."

Rachel brought them out and handed them over.

Kelly regarded her gratefully. "I appreciate you doing this for the school."

Rachel smiled. "And I appreciate the sparkle you've brought to my son's eye."

Taken aback, Kelly sputtered, "I haven't…"

Dan's mother raised her hand. "Please. It's been two

years since he left Chicago and came back to Laramie. Not that my son doesn't have the right to be bitter about what happened there. Honestly, after the way his life blew up both personally and professionally, I wasn't sure he'd ever want to get serious about settling down again."

Was this about a woman? And if so, who? Kelly struggled to understand. "From what I've heard, Dan made it clear that he *did* want that. It's why he had, er, has such an active social life." And also why as far as she was concerned, he may as well have had a big red warning sign plastered across his impossibly broad chest.

"Oh believe me, I'm very much aware of how my son has behaved." Rachel sighed, concern in her eyes. "He's spent time with an entire parade of eligible women. And found every single one of them lacking as a potential spouse, after just one or two outings! Until you…"

The romantic side of Kelly wanted to make something of that. However, the practical side of her forced her to point out sagely, "Yes, Dan and I have been hanging out together, a lot lately, for a whole host of reasons, but as far as an official courtship, we just had the one date."

Although they had also managed to see each other or talk at least once, if not multiple times, every day since she'd first approached him about helping her. Not to mention she thought, her face heating at the memory, kissed numerous times and recklessly made love!

Rachel led the way back down the staircase. "And in that time you—and your adorable triplets—are all Dan talks about. You're also the first woman he's brought out to the ranch he grew up on since his relationship with Belinda blew up in his face."

Belinda? Who was Belinda?

Rachel sobered. "The fact he wanted you to meet us counts for something, Kelly."

Did it? She wanted to believe that. Especially because she hadn't met her former in-laws until after the elopement, and unlike this, that meeting had not gone well. Not at all.

Unfortunately, to her frustration, she and Rachel had no more chance to talk privately since it was clear from the sounds of a truck pulling up in front of the ranch house that the men were back. The two women headed down to the foyer just as Dan and Frank came back in the front door. Despite the heat, looking none the worse for wear after the strenuous chore.

"I told Dan he can keep the trailer in his barn until you need the folding tables and chairs this weekend," Frank informed her kindly. "That way you won't have to load and unload it twice."

Still holding the stack of linens, Kelly nodded. "Thank you so much. I really appreciate this. And I know the school will, too."

Rachel and Frank stood together, arm in arm, the epitome of marital bliss. "It was our pleasure," they informed her with a smile, then Rachel handed Dan the prepacked cooler she'd had waiting in the foyer.

Goodbyes said, Dan and Kelly walked out. He inclined his head at the closed trailer attached to the back of his truck. "Do we have time to swing by the ranch to drop off the trailer and the food my mom packed for me before we head back into town?"

Kelly glanced at her watch, aware it was just after eight thirty. "Yes." Plenty, actually, to her delight. "My sitter isn't expecting me back until around eleven."

She lifted a staying hand before he could read more into her preemptory decision than there was. She hadn't made those arrangements so they would have time to make love. As much as the notion excited her. She had made them to ensure she had time to do all she needed for the preschool picnic.

"I figured it would take a lot longer to load the stuff." That she and Dan would be doing the heavy lifting, not him and his dad.

He flashed her a sexy grin. "So noted. But if you're game, we could hang out at the ranch. Maybe have a little dessert?"

It was an innocent invitation. Given with the kind of easy camaraderie she'd come to expect from him. Hoping it might lead to the kind of enduring friendship she wanted to have with him, Kelly smiled and said, "I'd like that." It would give them time to talk. Which was good. She wanted to feel close to him.

Plus, there was still an awful lot she'd like to know about him, and his past, and the heartache he'd apparently suffered during his time away from Texas.

Chapter Nine

Dan had not needed Kelly to pick up the folding tables and chairs. He easily could have texted photos for her approval—the same with the coordinating linens—and moved them over to his place for safekeeping. But he had asked her to go because he had wanted her to see she would be welcomed by his parents in a way she hadn't been by her ex-husband's.

He hadn't expected her to come out of that casual introduction so unsettled, though. Her quiet mood worried him a little. He'd expected the meeting with his parents to help their relationship along. "Everything okay?"

"Yes." She leaned back in the passenger seat and watched him back the trailer into the barn. "Why do you ask?"

He hopped out to unhook it, shut the barn doors, then got back in to drive his truck over to the ranch house. "You haven't said much since we left my parents' ranch."

She made a soft, noncommittal sound. "I was thinking about something your mother said."

He bit down on a curse. And here they went. "Which was…?" He circled around to hold her door open for her.

She climbed out, smiling a little at his gallantry.

"That you had every right to be bitter after the way your life blew up there."

The thing was, his bitterness had faded—not when he'd moved back home to Laramie, as he had expected—but when he had met Kelly, and decided he wanted to go out with her. Dan grabbed the cooler and carried it into the house, turning on lights as he went. Kelly followed him into the kitchen and at his invitation settled down on an island stool. Kelly's expression was so concerned, he had to ask. "Did she tell you the whole story?"

"Just that she had worried you wouldn't ever be really ready to settle down again."

Initially, he hadn't been.

Dan opened the cooler and brought out labeled packages, putting some in the freezer, a few in the fridge. One, he kept out on the counter.

He frowned, irritated by his mom's meddling. Going back to the fridge, he got out a can of whipped cream. "You'd think I hadn't recently bought a ranch with a seven-bedroom house."

She tilted her head. "You don't have to talk about it."

He begged to differ. "Clearly, my mother wants me to." Kelly, too, if he was reading her mood accurately.

"Yeah, well…"

He brought two plates and two forks over to her, along with a huge piece of his mother's decadent triple chocolate layer cake. He cut it in half and plated each.

It was hard to address her fears when he didn't know precisely what had been revealed. "Yeah, well, what?" he prodded.

Kelly flushed. "I had the feeling she assumed I already knew that you'd been serious about another woman and that it had ended badly."

He paused to put a generous amount of whipped cream on each piece of cake. "Relationships always end badly." He took the stool next to hers. "Otherwise they wouldn't end."

Kelly moaned in ecstasy as she took her first bite of cake. "Oh my goodness, this is amazing."

"I know. My mom can really bake."

"No kidding."

For a moment, they savored the confection in blissful silence.

He had just started to hope Kelly would be permanently distracted when she turned. Her full lips pursed as she studied him carefully. "She said something about your professional life exploding, too."

He blew out a breath, some of the pain he'd felt then coming back to haunt him. "Got to hand it to Mom. She really covered all the bases."

Kelly licked some chocolate off the back of the spoon with the same slow sensual intensity with which she made love. "I think she just wants you to be happy. And," Kelly added, waving her spoon and beginning to frown, "*she* thinks the fact we had one date and have been keeping company could be the beginning to that."

Dan grinned. "She could be right."

"Don't you start." Kelly stood. Carried her empty plate to the sink.

He picked up his and joined her. "Feeling pressured?" He rested his hands on her shoulders. Knowing if he were to be successful in wooing her, they'd have to go at her speed.

Tilting her head up to his, she glared. Correcting, "Feeling like there is a whole lot I still don't know about you. Might never know. And that worries me."

Dan understood not wanting to be blindsided in a relationship. He took her hand and led her to the L-shaped sectional. When they'd settled, he asked pensively, "Where do you want me to start?"

She drew a tremulous breath. "Chicago. How and why did you end up there?"

Figuring she needed to know this, he put his hand on hers. "I wanted to go somewhere different. Where the name McCabe didn't mean what it did in Texas. I really needed to prove myself, and there were opportunities for me to more swiftly achieve the rank of detective there."

Her fingers slid into his. "And did you?"

He looked down at their entwined hands. Her palm heated beneath his. He loved the silky warmth of her skin.

Dan nodded. "Within three years, thanks to my dual degrees in criminal justice and forensic accounting."

As their eyes met, he felt warmed through and through, which eased some of the tension he felt bubbling beneath the surface. "Did you like it?"

Dan focused on the good times. "Initially, yes. I like solving puzzles. And in the white collar crime division, it can take a lot of digging to uncover money laundering and embezzlement. Fraud. So there were plenty of challenges."

She rubbed her bare knee along the outer seam of his jeans. "How long were you there?"

Lord, she was sexy. Wondering if she had any idea the effect she had on him, he returned gruffly, "Six years."

Kelly sat back. Curious. "So what happened to blow it all up?"

Dan figured he might as well get it all out before someone else in his family told her. Grimacing, he reflected, "I met Belinda. She came to me because she thought something was going on at the investment company her father co-owned, that he was being threatened in some way."

"Sounds scary."

It had been. "She certainly got my sympathy." He scowled. "Not too long after that, an accountant who worked for the company turned up dead in what was supposed to look like a suicide, but clearly wasn't."

"That sounds even worse."

"Yeah, well, it was, and Belinda was really frightened for her whole family. She leaned on me. I felt for her and wanted to protect her."

She cocked her head. "And then became romantically involved?"

Now, the hard part. "Yes. And I shouldn't have. I mean, technically we weren't investigating Belinda and she wasn't involved with the company in any way, but it was still a line I shouldn't have crossed."

"Why did you?" The irises of her eyes turned a darker amber.

"I thought I was in love with her."

They sat for a moment in silence. "But you weren't."

Was that relief he saw? "In the end, I realized I didn't know her at all."

Another silence, this one even more fraught with emotion. "What about Belinda's dad? Did you feel a similar empathy for him?"

"No. From the first, I felt like he might be involved in what turned out to be a giant Ponzi scheme."

The tension in her shoulders eased slightly. "I'm guessing you had to investigate him."

He nodded. "I was part of a team scrutinizing the entire company and everyone who worked there, especially the executives."

She touched his arm compassionately. "That must have been tough if you were involved with Belinda."

Loving the warmth and softness of her, as much as the understanding in her lovely eyes, Dan said, "For me, yes, it was difficult. For her," he recalled grimly, "it was an advantage. Belinda wanted me to keep her informed, so her dad and his cohorts could stay one step ahead of the investigation."

Kelly sucked in a shocked breath, looking as protective of him as he felt of her. "And did you?" she asked.

Aware what a good wife she would make, he paused to let his gaze rove over her face. "Wear a wire? And feed Belinda false information? And record all our conversations on the matter? Yeah," he admitted triumphantly, "I did."

Kelly drew in a swift, shocked breath, the action lifting—then lowering—the soft swell of her breasts. "What happened?"

His need to make love to this beautiful, amazing woman again intensified. "Her dad was cleared of all involvement in the murder of the accountant, but he did go to prison for his part in the rest of it. Belinda cut an immunity deal with the district attorney in exchange for her testimony against her father and his partners in crime."

"Oh, Dan." Kelly's voice broke as she wrapped her arms around him, reminding him what a sweet and compelling lover she was. "I'm sorry."

He savored her silky warmth and tenderness. "I'm not," he murmured against her hair. Drawing back, he told her, "Everything that happened there made me reevaluate my life. Think about what I wanted and needed. Where I wanted to be."

Kelly smiled. "Here, in Texas, with your family."

Where there was no need to be as cynical and guarded

as he had eventually become, back in Chicago. He nodded, already feeling the legendary McCabe optimism begin to return.

"And you," he told her softly, shifting her onto his lap and bringing her closer still. He threaded his hands through her hair. "From the very first moment I laid eyes on you, Kelly, I wanted you to be mine." And that instinct had only gotten stronger, he thought, as he took her in his arms and kissed her long and hard and deep. Eager to touch her again, he eased his palms beneath the hem of her T-shirt, over her ribs, to the plump undersides of her breasts. She shivered and his thumbs rasped her hardened nipples.

She kissed him back fervently, her hands skimming over his back, shoulders, then down across his abs, to his belt.

Body hardening, he paused. Not wanting to rush her again. "Hey," he said softly, lifting her hand and kissing the inside of her wrist. Wanting her to know he could be as patient as she needed him to be. "I'm okay if you just want to focus on getting to know each other first."

Her eyes grew misty. "I know."

His own body humming with desire, he dropped his hold on her and continued frankly, "If you want to opt out of anything sexy, now's the time."

She hitched in a breath and said even more softly, sweetly, "I know that, too."

"But?"

She curled her palms around his biceps and regarded him wistfully, her determination to control the situation stronger than ever. "I haven't ever wanted anyone the way I do you. And now that I do…" She shrugged, suddenly looking a little shy.

He understood, having suffered a similar drought. "You want to just go with it?" He sure as heck did.

"And forget all about boundaries…" She undid his zipper, moved her hand south.

The feel of her hand closing in nearly sent him spiraling into oblivion. Groaning, he caught her wrist, not about to get that far ahead of her. "Let's slow down…" So they could make love again the way they were meant to, slowly and meaningfully.

She grinned saucily. "Hmm… I say, 'Let's not.'"

Dan could see if they wanted their coming together to be as good as it could be, he was going to have to take matters into his own hands. Not let her rush them in and out of bed, again. "Uh-huh." He stood, pulling her with him. Sliding a hand beneath her knees, he lifted her against his chest and proceeded toward the stairs.

She appeared to like the romantic gesture as much as he'd hoped. "This could become a habit," she warned playfully, nuzzling his neck.

Savoring the feel of her in return, he inhaled her sultry perfume. "One I'd surely like to have."

She laughed softly as he reached his room and then lowered her slowly, deliberately next to the bed. It was clear from the ardent look in her eyes she knew exactly what she wanted and needed from him. From this. "Now where were we?" he rasped, his entire body hardening.

She wreathed her arms about his neck and went up on tiptoe, eager to show him. "How about here?"

A delectably sweet kiss followed.

Desire pulsing in his loins, he eased off her T-shirt and bra. "Or here." He claimed her velvety softness, weighing and palming the feminine globes and taut crowns.

"Or here." She eased off his shirt, too. Pressing the softness of her breasts against the hardness of his chest.

And still they kissed and kissed.

Her knees weakening, slender body swaying, even as his lower half throbbed. Her hands went to his fly, and this time he let her find him. She sighed with pleasure as her fingers tantalized.

Impatient now, he unhooked her shorts, slid his hands beneath elastic and eased everything off.

She chuckled. "Not getting ahead of me there, cowboy," she said, doing the same for him.

Naked, they came together again. "Now where were we?" he quipped.

"Not to worry," she murmured, molding her warm body to his, her pretty face alight with the promise of pleasure. "I'm not about to lose my place."

"Right back at you, cowgirl." Still kissing her thoroughly, he danced her backward, tumbling them both onto the bed. Emotions soaring, heart racing, he stretched over top of her, holding her wrists on either side of her. Then slowly made his way down, kissing, caressing as he went.

She arched up off the bed, trembling. "Um… Dan…?"

Not about to be satisfied with anything less than full surrender, he stroked her with the pads of his thumbs until her breath was rasping and the air between them vibrated with excitement and escalating desire. "Hmm?"

He loved the heat of her body, the way she strained against him. Still struggling to maintain a modicum of control, even as she gasped, "I don't know if you can call me cowgirl since I don't know anything about living on a ranch."

She already knew a lot about pleasing—and responding—to him, though. "No problem." He settled between her thighs, wrapping his arms around them, holding her limbs apart. Dipping his head again, he promised softly, "I'll teach you everything you need to know…"

Kelly had figured if they could make their coming together quick and hot and dirty, like last time, she would also be able to keep her inner vulnerability at bay. But as in synch with her feelings as ever, Dan wasn't about to let her play it this way.

He wanted her, heart and soul.

And held against him this way, at the mercy of his erotic ministrations, it was impossible to pretend she could keep this—keep them—in unromantic territory. At least while they were in bed. And she did want to be in bed with him, she realized, as sensations ran riot inside her. She did want to make love. Here. Now. Oh heavens above… He was making her feel not just wanted, but needed. More tantalizing still, the tingles soaring through her had her quivering and arching up off the bed. "Um… Dan?" she said again, in a slight panic as his tongue made lazy circles, moved up, in.

She was not going to let him convince her to do something really reckless and fall in love with him.

She wasn't…

"Hmmmm?" Exploring tenderly, he pushed her closer, closer to the brink.

Unable to help it, she made that low sound of acquiescence in her throat that she knew he loved. She shuddered again, as he continued to lay claim the way only he could. Slowly. Inevitably. Patiently. She moaned again, even more deliriously this time. Then panted, "I think you already are. Teaching me, that is…"

He grinned against her skin, the low sound of triumph in his voice. He found the sweet sensitive spot with the pad of his thumb. Her head fell back and he continued the intimate stroking. "Some things come naturally."

Rocking slightly, she surged, until there was no doubt about what she wanted, what they both wanted, had to have. Shuddering with the sweetest yearning she'd ever felt, she fisted her hands in his hair, gasping playfully, "You're right. Some things are fated. And I want you inside me when I come." Which was about to be any second.

She didn't have to ask twice. He found a condom, rolled it on and then stretched over top of her. He slid his hands beneath her, lifting her. "Like this?"

How she wanted him to possess her! She wrapped her legs about his waist, open and ready. Trembling with anticipation, whispered back, "Just like this." She looked deep into his eyes.

He slid home with one smooth, deep stroke. And then there was no more playful messing around, no more holding back. Only wet hot kisses and white-hot possession. Unimaginable pleasure and searing release.

When it was over, Dan kissed Kelly's shoulder and cuddled her close.

As she'd expected, worry soon mingled with the contentment flowing inside her.

"You're awfully pensive," he said finally.

She savored his warmth and his strength while he stroked a hand through the silk of her hair. "So are you."

He pressed a kiss against her temple. "What are you thinking?"

She bit her lip, as the barriers between them began to re-erect. She lifted her head to stare into his eyes. "Honestly?"

He nodded, serious now. "Nothing but."

Kelly knew pretending wouldn't help. Whether he liked it or not, he needed to know how she felt. She sat up dragging the sheet with her, holding it to her breasts.

"That all this is too good to be true." *And that I hate feeling vulnerable, like the whole world might crash in on me again at any second and steal what happiness I've found.*

She started to get up. He reeled her back in. Waited.

She swallowed at the effort it took to meet his dark assessing gaze. "I'm not going to say I didn't enjoy it."

Finally a smile, albeit just a hint of one. He rubbed the pad of his thumb across her cheek. "Good." He gave her a lazy once-over, admitting huskily, "Because I loved every minute of it, too."

The lovemaking.

Not her.

Which was yet another sign they needed to keep this affair—if that's what it was—in the strictly friends with benefits category.

Kelly inhaled a bolstering breath. "But I'm also not going to say I trust this to last."

With the exception of her triplets, the good moments in her life never did.

Dan shook his head. His expression patient, but grim. "There we differ."

She knew the dreams he had. Of enjoying an enduring marriage, like his folks. Of filling up this great big gorgeous home with a half dozen kids.

But they weren't hers.

Not now.

Maybe not ever. "I don't want to get married, Dan. Not again. And we both know you do."

He nodded, for once not trying to persuade her otherwise. Although she had the feeling he was about to when a shrill baaing and hysterical barking split the silent night air.

Alarmed, Dan raced naked to the window and peered

out into the courtyard. There was just enough light spilling from the porch lamps for him to see.

"Trouble?"

Grimly, he reached for his jeans. "Like you wouldn't believe."

Chapter Ten

"What is it?" Kelly asked, her heart pounding at the alarm on Dan's face.

"Looks like a family of raccoons!" He jerked on his boots and raced out the door. Kelly dressed as quickly as possible and followed.

By the time she got outside, the furry gray, black and white animals were scurrying across the field, toward a wooded area between the perimeters of Bowie Creek and a neighboring ranch. Shep was still racing back and forth, barking, torn between following the invading critters or guarding the mini goats, now roaming freely around the grassy expanse of the small ranch.

The dirt had been dug up next to the tall fence surrounding the goat pen, leaving a nice big escape burrow.

Dan pointed to the goats. "Round 'em up, Shep!"

Glad for the instruction, his dog gave a happy bark and then raced toward the goats now heading off into the moonlit darkness. "What can I do to help?" Kelly asked.

He shot her an appreciative glance. "Get the leather leads on the hook just inside the barn door and bring them out." He strode in that direction, too. "I'll get a shovel and close this hole up."

For the next ten minutes, they worked in silence. The bare-chested Dan shoveled, an action, Kelly couldn't help but note, that nicely delineated the sculpted muscles in his back and shoulders. Shep rounded the goats up and expertly herded them back in the direction of the pen. Kelly snapped on leads one at a time and brought the runaway animals back to the enclosure.

Finally, all was calm again.

Shep collapsed on the ground, panting. With an amiable grin, Dan walked over to pet him. "Good job, fella."

Feeling like she had just run a marathon, too, Kelly knelt on the other side of him and praised the collie, as well. "We couldn't have done it without you, buddy."

Shep thumped his tail and leaned into their touches. Kelly and Dan exchanged looks and smiles of relief.

While in the pen, the goats drank and ate the last of the dinner feed in their trough.

Together, Kelly and Dan mounted the steps to the ranch house. He bumped a broad shoulder to hers, and she gazed up into his warm blue eyes. As always, his closeness did something funny low in her belly.

"I guess I owe you a debt of gratitude, too," he told her. "For helping me with this latest goat catastrophe."

She leaned into the arm he laced about her shoulders. Trying once again not to think what a good team they made. In and out of bed. "Were the raccoons trying to attack the goats?"

Shaking his head, Dan held the door for her. "Most likely they just wanted the food." He followed her inside, his steps long and lazy. "But now we've got a real problem because they know where the goat feed is." He paused to wash his forearms and hands, then headed for the fridge.

Kelly stopped at the sink, too. "They'll be back?"

He pulled out two bottles of blue Gatorade and when

she had finished drying her hands, handed her one. "Oh, yeah. No question."

Kelly unscrewed the top and drank thirstily. She lounged against the kitchen counter, tense with worry. "What are you going to do?"

Looking incredibly sexy in just jeans and boots, he said, "Call in reinforcements."

By the time Kelly had restored order to her hair and makeup and Dan had finished getting dressed, help had indeed arrived. And this time there was nothing for Kelly to do but hang out on the front porch with Shep and watch.

With the assistance of two of his brothers—Matt, a military veteran, and Chase, a saddle company executive—Dan lit the perimeter surrounding the miniature-goat pen with flashlights and camping lanterns. Matt, who'd apparently had a similar problem on his ranch, had also brought humane traps and bait. Chase, who also owned a nearby ranch, had a roll of twelve-inch-wide steel mesh that could be slid into the ground along the outside perimeter of the pen.

When they'd finished, Dan asked, "You guys mind hanging out here for an hour or so to keep an eye on things so I can drive Kelly home?"

"Depends," Chase said with a grin, as he and Matt eyed first their brother then Kelly in a way that made her think they knew exactly how bad she and Dan had it for one another.

Knew, and approved.

It was a nice feeling, knowing that in the Frank and Rachel McCabe clan she would be accepted—the way she never had been in her ex's. But it scared her, too. Because without such hurdles in their way, how would she do what she had promised herself from the beginning: manage to keep the walls around her heart intact?

THE NEXT MORNING, Kelly stared at the coloring project given to them by the school art instructor. "You've got to be kidding me. *Another* Father's Day decoration?"

This one was all letters spelling out Happy Father's Day! "Did the director approve this?"

Her fellow three-year-old-class teacher, Cece Taylor, grimaced. "I don't think she had much of a choice. Mirabelle and company are putting so much pressure on her to at least equal the festivity quotient of the Mother's Day Tea."

Which had not gone over well with those who had no maternal figure in their lives.

Rhonda, the art teacher, said, "The director's thinking is that the kids can't read, so...we don't necessarily have to tell them what they are coloring."

Her temper rising, Kelly stared at the papers. "But the parents—or remaining parent—can!"

"I know," Rhonda whispered, being careful not to be overheard by any of the students involved in free play in the large classroom's game and toy area. "And I feel for you. But think of it this way. This whole mess will be over soon, and we won't have to deal with it again until next May. So..."

"I agree," Cece said. "Let's just let Mirabelle win this one, and then maybe she'll back off a little."

Fat chance, Kelly thought, then paused. All three teachers watched as Shoshanna trudged in. The little girl looked like she had lost her best friend. "Oh, dear," Cece murmured.

Oh, dear was right, Kelly thought. She made her way over to the morose little girl's side. Kneeling to help the child get her backpack off, she asked, "How is your mom feeling today, honey?" Kelly hoped Sharon wasn't still feverish and throwing up.

Shoshanna shrugged.

"Did she bring you to school?"

For a moment, Shoshanna looked as if she were going to burst into tears. Finally, she said, "My babysitter did."

"Is your mommy going back to work today?"

"She already did," Shoshanna pouted. "Before I even went to school."

Gently, Kelly prodded, "Is that why you're sad?"

Another desultory shake of the head. "I'm sad because Mommy's sad."

That made sense, Kelly thought, her heart going out to them both. Children were always quick to pick up and take on the mood in a home. No matter what it was.

Shoshanna's lower lip trembled anxiously. "She's always sad when she talks to the little man."

Doing her best not to show her alarm, Kelly said, "The little man?"

Another nod. Tears glittered on Shoshanna's eyelashes. "He always makes her sad," she revealed petulantly, crossing her arms over her chest. "So I don't like him."

Neither did Kelly. Whoever he was. She gave her student's hands a reassuring squeeze. "But your mommy was okay when she went to work, right?"

Again, Shoshanna hesitated. "Just…tired."

That wasn't much to go on. But it definitely warranted a call, Kelly thought, as the soft beginning of the day chime sounded.

Kelly led the Morning Circle—a routine of familiar songs and the school friendship pledge—then got the kids in her class settled, with their coloring activity. With Cece, Rhonda and a few volunteer moms momentarily watching both classes, she stepped into the hall. Calls to Sharon went unanswered, so she telephoned Dan—who was still out at his ranch, dealing with the aftermath of the raccoon problem.

"I'm worried," she said after she had caught him up on the latest developments regarding Sharon and Shoshanna.

"You want to call in social services?" He spoke above the racket of the bleating mini goats and what sounded like several motor vehicle engines.

"No! I want you to find out who the little man is who is upsetting them!"

"I can barely hear. Let me step inside the ranch house." The racket faded. A door shut. Finally, Dan spoke. "Did Shoshanna indicate there had been any kind of emotional or physical abuse going on?"

"Not directly, no, but..." Kelly gulped, her feelings in turmoil. "Isn't there something you can do—some kind of detective work or something—to protect them from...harm?"

"From what you've told me, it isn't really a law-enforcement matter."

Not yet. Kelly rubbed the tense muscles in her forehead. "What if it becomes one?"

"Then we'll deal with it promptly," Dan promised.

"And until then?"

"Under the law—"

Which was what Dan was sworn to go by, Kelly realized, even as disappointment flowed through her.

"—Sharon is entitled to her privacy."

Kelly knew he was right. Even as she knew she couldn't stand by and do nothing when one of her students was clearly in such emotional distress. So when the day came to an end and she still hadn't heard back from Sharon, Kelly arranged for her children to have a last-minute playdate with some of their friends, took matters into her own hands and headed for the auto dealership where Sharon worked.

WHEN THE MINI-GOAT situation was finally taken care of, Dan showered and headed for the auto dealership.

Somehow, he wasn't surprised to see Kelly inside the glass-walled showroom, checking out the tires on a brand-new SUV.

Even though it was the end of a workday for her, she looked ridiculously beautiful. Her caramel hair was delectably tousled, her lips soft and bare, her cheeks a becoming pink. She was clad in sandals and a cap-sleeved sundress that fell to just above her knees. It was clear from the way the cotton was clinging almost damply to her breasts that she was overheated.

Desire sent an arrow of fire to his groin. Desire, he did not want to feel, not there, and not then.

Irritated she'd ignored his dictum, he strode in, for the moment bypassing the row of offices he was supposed to be heading for. Stopped just short of her, and letting his glance drift over the supple length of her, said, "Fancy meeting you here."

Their gazes clashed. Stubbornly, she held her ground. "I could say the same about you."

"Mmm-hmm," he countered.

It was clear from the guilty look on her face that she was here to snoop. An act that he knew, from experience, would only make things worse. He stepped closer still. "I really think you should leave this to the professionals."

A half-dozen emotions—none of them welcoming to him—crossed her face. She folded her arms in front of her, insisting, just as resolutely, "Believe me, Dan, I am all too aware of your feelings on the subject. But I am personally invested in this, and I want to be involved…"

"Involved with what?" a familiar feminine voice said behind him.

They turned in unison.

Sharon Johnson stood in a business suit and heels, the name tag identifying her as director of financial services, pinned to her lapel. Her hair was nicely done as always, but her makeup was different. The base color looked like it had been put on with a very heavy hand. Although the application of cheek and lip and eye color seemed normal.

Dan could tell by the way Kelly's eyes had widened in surprise that she had noticed the telltale difference, too.

Meanwhile, Sharon looked from Dan to Kelly and then back again. Dan noted that the woman looked as if she were suffering from the uncommon heat inside the building, too.

So it wasn't just his reaction to Kelly.

Or Kelly's to him.

"Or shouldn't I ask?" Sharon prodded lightly, hands on her hips.

Determined to lighten the mood for all their sakes, Dan shrugged and cut Kelly a chastising glance. "You might as well tell her, honey."

As he expected, the public endearment surprised Kelly and threw her off. She opened her mouth, started to say something, then stopped and shook her head. Sweetly, she threw the ball back in his court. "Honestly, *honey*, I think you should be the one to explain why we're both here at the very same time. Especially after the conversation we had earlier today."

Why did he suddenly feel as if he were involved in a "marital" tiff?

They weren't that close yet, no matter how much he wanted to be. Were they?

The challenge in Kelly's eyes had Dan turning back to Sharon. He called on as much of the truth as he could muster. "Kelly found out I've never had anything but a gray or silver vehicle, and she doesn't think I should go with the same color again. So, I asked her what she thought might be best..."

"And I told him," Kelly cut in, "that since in the end he is the one who is going to have to live with this, that it really is his decision."

Sharon tilted her head in confusion.

Someone opened the door to their left. Another blast of sweltering mid-June heat poured inside the showroom.

Moisture beaded along Sharon's cheek. She lifted a hand to blot it. Damp makeup shifted from her skin onto her fingers, exposing a visible dark red area beneath.

Dan noted the detail like a punch to his gut but remained stoic. Kelly reacted with obvious shock and dismay.

Sharon tracked Kelly's glance. Blushing, she spun around on her heel. "Sorry. If you'll excuse me." She ducked into the closest ladies' room.

Kelly darted in after her.

Hoping she didn't make things worse, Dan went to talk to the salesperson handling his transaction.

The papers were ready, so it took only fifteen minutes to sign them and hand over a check.

"Should be here, two days, max," the salesperson said.

Dan shook his hand. "Thanks."

Without warning, Kelly appeared beside him. Sharon was coming up behind her. He could tell Kelly was shaken by whatever had transpired in the ladies' room, but was clearly trying not to show it.

He shrugged. "Sorry, honey, I went with the silver exterior and gray interior again."

She smiled, pretending that really was the reason she had showed up at the dealership. "I figured." She put her hand on his arm. "I didn't mean to interrupt. I just wanted to let you know I was leaving."

"I'll come with you." He walked her as far as the sidewalk outside before she turned and gave him a faux pleasant look. "I don't want to talk here."

They could both see Sharon—as well as a few others—watching them through the plate-glass windows. "Where then?" he said just as pleasantly.

Her amber eyes darkened. A pulse throbbed in the hollow of her throat as she countered in a low, hoarse voice, "My house. We'll have about fifteen minutes before the kids are dropped off."

Dan didn't care where they went as long as they had the privacy they needed to hash this out. "Sounds good."

She got in her car. He got in his, then followed her to her place. She paused only long enough to get her mail from the box at the curb, then led the way inside. Grimacing in concern, she swung back to face him. "You saw the red marks on Sharon's face?"

He nodded. As their eyes met and held, he felt a shimmer of tension between them. Man-woman tension. "As well as the heavy application of makeup."

The window blinds had been closed during the day to keep out the midday heat and sun. Now, she went around, opening them. "Sharon said it is rosacea, a form of menopausal acne, that's exacerbated by illness and stress." She heaved a commiserating sigh. "Both of which she's had a lot of lately."

He studied the conflicted look on Kelly's face. "Do you believe her?"

"I don't know. I mean, it could be."

"But…?"

Kelly wrung her hands. "She didn't quite look me in the eye when she was telling me about it."

"That could be from embarrassment," Dan pointed out in an effort to keep them both from jumping to ill-formed conclusions.

"Instead of evasion or an attempt to hide something else," Kelly guessed.

He nodded. A contemplative silence fell. As he looked into her eyes, he picked up a myriad of sentiments. Concern. Curiosity. The need to protect. As well as understand. She was a good and generous woman who meant well, but because they didn't quite know yet what they were dealing with, could easily make a mistake. One that might make things worse for everyone.

He stepped closer, momentarily resisting the urge to take her in his arms. "If it helps, I didn't see any swelling, and usually if someone has been hit, or had a fall especially within the last forty-eight hours, there would be swelling."

"I didn't see any, either."

"And yet…?"

Kelly perched on the back of the sofa. "I want to believe I'm overreacting unnecessarily." She bit her lip uncertainly.

Dan tried not to notice the way her skirt rode up slightly on her thigh. "But…?" he prodded.

Kelly planted her hands on either side of her. Softly, regretfully, she admitted, "I've been mistaken before when it comes to reading people I care about, and what is really going on with them. I turned a blind eye when I shouldn't have. Mostly, because I really wanted and hoped everything was okay." Shaking her head, she swallowed and pushed on, "Then later, when it all went to hell, I really regretted not trusting my gut instinct in the first place." She smoothed a hand over the soft cotton fabric of her work dress. "Because maybe if I had…" Her personal misery seemed to increase tenfold.

He settled on the sofa beside her. "You're talking about your mother?"

"And my ex-husband. His very unwelcoming family…"

She had been through way too much. Needing to comfort her the way she hadn't been in the past, Dan put his arm around her shoulders. "When it came to your mother and her disease, you were a kid. You were too young to know how to handle her addiction." He waited until she looked him in the eye before he continued compassionately, "When it came to your ex, you were still awfully young, and no more prepared to deal with that kind of greed and manipulation than I was when I got involved with Belinda. So I think we should both give ourselves passes on our mutual gullibility and any mistakes we made back then. Deal?"

She smiled. "Deal."

Determined to soothe her, he continued, "As far as Sharon goes, she's clearly struggling, and her little girl is picking up on that, but I'm not getting the vibe that she is the victim of any kind of domestic disturbance." Yet, anyway. And, as a veteran law officer, he had been trained to pick up on that.

Still conflicted, Kelly wrested herself from his embrace and walked away. She shoved her hands through her hair, pushing the silky strands away from her face. "Then what else could be going on with them?" She began to pace. "Because I tell you, Dan, I know it's something!"

He took a moment to consider. "Is it possible she's quarreling with extended family? Or maybe even her late husband's family? Having custody or visitation issues?"

"She hasn't mentioned anything. I mean, I was under the impression from what she said and the preschool admission papers she filled out that there wasn't anyone else. That it was just her and her daughter."

Dan followed her to the kitchen where she continued opening blinds. "When you were talking with her at the dealership, did you ask her about the little man her daughter referenced?" he asked, noting the way the sunlight streaming in caught the highlights in her hair. He had a sudden urge to feel the silky strands between his fingertips. "The one who always made her cry?"

She went into the mudroom. Delicate hand braced on the wooden lockers there, she exchanged her heeled work sandals for a pair of hot pink flip-flops. "I wanted to, but I worried doing so would push her away, make her shut down. And I think she needs friends here as much as her little girl does."

"That could be true of all of us."

Kelly straightened, one hand smoothing the skirt of her sundress. "So what do we do?"

Sensing Kelly needed comforting as much as she needed backup in this situation, he placed his arms about her waist and drew her all the way against him. "We remain on standby. Let her know we're here for her, if she needs us." He gazed at her soft lips. "And then hope if she does, she will come to us."

Kelly sighed and smiled. She splayed her hands across his chest. "You are such a great guy, you know that?"

Dan ran one hand over her spine. He cupped her chin with the other. Huskily, he admitted, "I know I like hearing it from you." His head lowering to deliver the kiss he sensed she wanted as much as he did, he said, "I like seeing it in your eyes even more…"

Their lips met, and she surrendered to the passion engulfing them both. He felt her vulnerability and need, as surely as he felt his own desire to make her his. She lifted her arms to wreathe around his neck, and her body melded to his. She moaned at the onslaught of pleasure inundating them both. Dug her hands into his shoulders and kissed him with an erotic sweetness beyond his wildest dreams. Satisfaction roaring through him, he savored the taste and feel of her until she whispered, "Oh, Dan… you always know how to make me feel better, no matter what the circumstance."

He knew because he couldn't get enough of her, either. Happiness flowing through him, he strung kisses along her jaw, her ear, the nape of her neck. "I aim to please…"

"I know." Catching his head in her hands, she held on to him. Quavering now, her response all the encouragement he required. "Believe me," she murmured, even more tenderly, "I know."

He tilted her face up to his and meshed his lips with hers. With a low moan of surrender, she went up on tiptoe and rocked against him. Giving him a glimpse of what it would be like if she really let go. Kissing him back ardently. Running her hands down his spine, past his waist. Pressing lower, lower still.

Who knew what would have happened had they not suddenly run out of time? And heard cheerful young voices as car doors opened and shut outside. In shared frustration, they drew apart. Flushing fiercely, Kelly rushed through the house to the front windows and hazarded a glance out the window, where her three adorable children were already racing up the front walk toward the door.

Dan was as happy to see them as he was sad to miss out on the opportunity to make love with Kelly again.

He also knew the time for passion would come.

He and Kelly would both see to it.

STILL FEELING DELICIOUSLY RAVISHED, and a little frustrated, too, Kelly watched with amusement as her triplets climbed all over their guest. "Deputy Dan! You're here! We missed you!"

Having taken the interruption in stride, he hugged them all, just the way a daddy would, and ruffled each one's hair in turn. "I missed you guys, too," he admitted fondly.

Matthew asked, "Are you going to have dinner with us?"

"It's our favorite!" Michael added. "Breakfast for dinner night!"

Talk about being put on the spot. Although, Kelly thought, her lips still tingling, that was, coincidentally, exactly what she wanted, too. "First of all, we don't know how Deputy Dan feels about having breakfast for dinner."

He flashed an affable grin. "Love it."

Good to know. Kelly tore her eyes from his. "Second, he might have to work tonight."

"I do," Dan said. "But I don't go on duty until nine. I've got the dusk until dawn shift this evening. So, if I'm invited, I'd love to stay."

Kelly realized she would love to have him. And she wasn't the only one.

The triplets headed to the snack drawer in the kitchen that held their after-school snack, small packets of Goldfish crackers and pretzel bites.

Michelle took two and walked over to Dan, wordlessly offering him one.

He accepted the pretzels with a kind "Thanks."

Michelle smiled and settled in a chair at the breakfast table, along with her two brothers. "Are you going to marry our mommy yet?"

In the midst of doling out juice boxes, Kelly started. "Michelle…!" she chided, embarrassed.

Importantly, Michael cut in. He turned to lecture his sister. "He can't. He has to take care of his goats."

Kelly was not sure what the two things had to do with each other. She did know Dan suddenly looked awfully serious.

He pulled up a chair so he was at eye level with the kids.

"Actually, I need to talk to you about the goats," Dan said.

Matthew's eyes widened. "Did they run away again and eat the garden?"

"No," Dan exhaled, his demeanor turning ever more serious. "But we had some animals try to steal the goats' food last night. And it made me realize with me gone so much working, half of the time at night when they are in the most jeopardy, that Shep and I aren't always going to be able to protect them…" He cleared his throat and hesitated for a few beats before continuing. "So I found them all a new home today, with the agriculture teacher at the high school. She has room for them on the ranch she shares with her family, and some farm and ranch club students at the high school have volunteered to help take care of them."

"So the goats won't be at your ranch anymore?" Michelle asked plaintively.

"No. But they will be safely housed on a big ranch where there are always a lot of people and cowboys around to watch over them. And I can still visit them, and so can you-all, if your mom says it is okay."

The triplets turned to her in unison. "Can we, Mommy?"

Kelly nodded. "Of course. But right now I need to make dinner and you-all should really take advantage of your backyard playtime."

The kids ran outside to their swing set and sandbox.

Arms folded in front of him, Dan watched through window. "They took that better than I thought they would."

Kelly nodded, glad he had handled it so well. "They can be very resilient. Plus, like most well-adjusted, well-behaved children, they're used to not having absolutely everything they want, when they want it." Even though the maternal part of her did sometimes wish she could give them a more complete family and the daddy they deserved.

Dan swung around to face her. "What about you?" he probed softly. "Are you used to it?"

Chapter Eleven

Kelly had never had everything she wanted as a kid, or an adult. The closest she had come was right now. With the triplets and her job and her new home in Laramie. Since her divorce, the idea of having a good man in her life to love her had not even been in the realm of possibility.

Until now.

Until Dan.

Although she wasn't sure, given the ease and speed with which Dan could cut ties, it should be an option.

She also didn't know why she was surprised Dan had given the miniature goats away. He had said that was his intent from the beginning. And last night the small herd had definitely been in danger. So had Shep. Had the raccoons been rabid or even just aggressive in their search for food, having them all enclosed in that pen might well have resulted in a bloody brawl that could easily have turned deadly.

And had he been on night patrol, as he was going to be this evening, he would have not been there to do anything about it.

Maybe if he'd been able to put them in the barn at night, it would have been different. But he and his brothers had said it would be too hot for them to be closed up there, in the stifling summer heat, and raccoons were known to dig their way into barns, too.

So it was a good practical decision on his part. And it had nothing to do with her, or her kids.

So why did it feel as if it did? As if she might be next, if she and the kids didn't fit his life, either?

He picked up on her apprehension, as well as the reason for it, and informed her gently, "Having the herd cared for by agriculture students who wanted to raise miniature goats and didn't have the one to two thousand dollars just to purchase two pet goats turned out to be a very good solution."

"Why two?" Kelly asked curiously.

He watched her loop an apron over her head and tie it at her waist. "They're herd animals. They have to have companionship to thrive. Luckily, I didn't have to farm them out two at a time, and was able to keep them all together."

"What about feeding them?"

He lounged against the opposite counter, hands braced on either side of him. "I donated that, too."

She smiled. "It's very generous of you."

He shrugged. "I'd have been feeding them anyway if they were here."

"Still…"

He gave her a long look. "It was the right thing to do, Kelly."

She supposed in the final analysis it was. Wishing he weren't so darn chivalrous, she went to the fridge and began getting out the ingredients for dinner. "Sounds like it's all worked out then."

That got a half-smile out of him. "Better than I could have hoped."

Telling herself it was all good, Kelly slipped into the

walk-in pantry and emerged with containers of flour, baking powder, salt and sugar.

He helped her set it all out, his strong fingers brushing hers in the process. His eyes fell on the stack of Happy Father's Day artwork on the counter. "What's this?"

Still tingling from the accidental touch of their hands, Kelly explained, "That is today's preschool coloring project."

He paused and looked down at her, taking the time to drink her in. "Did all the kids do them?"

"Yes." They were standing so close she could feel the heat emanating from his powerful body. She found herself wanting to kiss him again.

He was distracted, too. His gaze touched over her features, before returning to her eyes. "Did it upset you?"

Kelly flushed as their gazes meshed. She measured dry ingredients in one bowl, then combined egg, milk, vanilla and canola oil in another. "Only in the sense that I know it's a warning shot across the bow from Mirabelle Evans." She pressed her lips together ruefully.

He lounged against the counter next to her, hands braced on either side of him. "What are you going to do about it?"

Kelly swallowed around the parched feeling in her throat and continued mixing the pancake batter. "Nothing I can do except carry on with my own plans to make the event next Saturday more of an annual June picnic than a celebration of what at least a third of the students at the school don't have."

He moved aside to give her room to work, assessing her with a glance. "What does Mirabelle say about the rectangular tables?"

"She doesn't know I have acquired any yet," Kelly

admitted, layering bacon slices in a baking pan and sliding it into the oven.

While Dan rinsed the strawberries, blueberries, raspberries and blackberries in the colander, Kelly brought out the vanilla yogurt and whipped cream to make parfaits.

He paused to take that in. "Are you planning to tell her?" Dan asked.

"Of course." Kelly cracked the ten remaining eggs into a bowl, added a small amount of water, then handed them over to Dan to whisk.

He squinted. "When?"

"On the day of the picnic when I show up with them."

He paused in mid-stir. Came closer yet. "You really think this is the best way to go about it?"

Trying not to think how well they worked together in the kitchen, almost as skillfully as they did in bed, Kelly set a skillet on the stove.

His disapproval rankled. "Look, you have no idea how much I've had to put up with from this woman."

He watched her turn the heat on under the griddle. "I get it. Mirabelle Evans is a pain."

Irritated he wasn't immediately taking her side in this, the way most boyfriends or husbands would do, Kelly huffed. "Worse than that, Dan. She's a Mean Girl. And then some." Kelly darkened as her outrage escalated. "The fact she wants to inflict damage to me—and the rest of the single parents in the preschool—is one thing. But when Mirabelle Evans goes after our kids, it's a game changer."

"You're not worried about the kids being caught in the middle of some big blowup between the two of you?"

His gruff sexy voice stirred her senses. Kelly lifted her chin. "Whose side are you on?"

He looked her in the eye. "In this case? The kids."

A contentious silence strung out between them.

The compassion in his glance faded, replaced by something much more acute. "I've been in law enforcement for a decade, Kelly." He regarded her intently. "I've seen what happens when people let their emotions—instead of cool reason—dictate their actions."

She glared at him. "And you think that's what I'm doing?"

He tilted his head, concern sharpening the edges of his face. "Don't you?"

Kelly threw up her hands, frustrated. "I've tried dealing with Mirabelle directly, Dan. We met privately for coffee after the Mother's Day Tea, at my invitation. I asked her very nicely if we could work together to find a way to celebrate Father's Day without hurting the kids who, for whatever reason, didn't currently have fathers in their lives."

"What did she say?"

"Nothing." Kelly checked on the bacon, then added eggs to the frying pan and dollops of pancake batter on the griddle. "She just smiled and said something like—" Kelly continued with acerbity "—it's too bad that more people didn't choose their life partners wisely. Instead of basing a marriage or relationship on something totally unreliable. Like passion—which never lasts. And then she walked away."

Finally, Dan understood. "Ouch." He took her hand in his.

"No kidding. Ouch." Kelly turned her glance away.

"I'm guessing her remarks cut very close to the bone."

Kelly sighed. "So deep that I'm still reeling from them."

He squinted. "Why do you care what Mirabelle thinks?"

Figuring he would never understand unless she explained, Kelly admitted miserably, "Because deep down, I know she's right. If I hadn't let my physical desire for my ex cloud my thinking, or let him convince me to run off and elope just as a big "So there!" to his controlling parents, I would never have entered an ill-fated union and gotten divorced. Never mind had children with a man who had no intention of ever being anything close to a loving father to them. But I did, so... I still have to deal. That doesn't however mean my kids have to be hurt, too," she said fiercely, balling her hands at her sides. "Or be made to feel, even indirectly, that they are something I should regret. Because I don't! My kids are the best thing that ever happened to me!" Her voice cracked emotionally, the way it always did when she found herself unable to completely protect them. Tears stung her eyes. She continued in a low, choked voice, "And I love them more than life."

"I know that, sweetheart." He pulled her against him for a long comforting hug. Inundating her with tenderness and warmth. "They love you, too!"

Silence fell. He let her have a moment to pull herself together.

"Which is maybe why," Dan continued gently, "you should consider putting an end to this feud with Mirabelle once and for all."

"Don't you think I've tried?" Kelly fumed, upset.

"Even after she gave me that snotty lecture on why it's important to be sensible and marry the right person," Kelly said, as she extricated herself from his arms and met his level gaze. "I did my best to take the high road. I backed off and gave Mirabelle Evans time to think about it, and hopefully reconsider, and you've seen the result. She's gone whole hog the other way."

Dan exhaled. Beginning to understand at long last the depth of animosity. "You think there's more?"

Kelly threw up her hands. Probably. "At this point I'm afraid to see what the decorations—which by the way are top secret, known only by the power moms on Mirabelle's party planning committee—are going to be like when we show up on Saturday to set up for the event."

"Which is perhaps even more reason to have it out with her now, *if* that is what you want to do."

Obviously, given the stern look on his handsome face, he did not think that was a wise course. Kelly poured batter on the buttered griddle, then spun back to face him. "So you think I should do what? Just surrender to Mirabelle's hurtful actions?" she countered emotionally, incensed.

"All I can tell you," Dan said wearily, abruptly looking like the lawman he was, at heart, "is that if I were you, I'd do whatever I could to make peace. As soon as possible. Before this situation really gets out of hand."

KELLY THOUGHT ABOUT what Dan said all through dinner and into the morning. And while the harmony-loving part of her certainly agreed with him, she still did not trust that there was any way to get her and Mirabelle Evans on the same page.

Which left her no choice but to put off the mom fireworks as long as possible, and hope by then that Mirabelle's need to triumph would be diluted by everything else that would likely be going on that day.

Meantime, she had to figure out how to restore the relaxed camaraderie between her and Dan McCabe. Their first disagreement had left her feeling a little down.

She was still ruminating over how to fix that when he phoned, just as she was getting off work. He sounded chipper, like he had woken up not long before. Which was probably true since he'd had the night shift the evening before. "Still ticked off at me?" Dan asked, his low familiar voice generating a riptide of warmth.

"You have a right to your opinion." And wasn't that what couples did? Hashed things out? Used each other as sounding boards? Gave each other advice, even when it wasn't exactly what the other person wanted to hear?

He exhaled, then continued in the low, gruffly sexy voice she loved. "Yeah, but, I shouldn't be butting in and telling you how to do your job, any more than I'd want you telling me how to do mine. So…peace?"

Glad they were once again on the same page, Kelly smiled and echoed, "Peace."

"Great!" He sounded as relieved and happy as she felt. "Are you busy this evening?"

Kelly paced back and forth on the school playground, letting the kids have one last romp before she piled them in the SUV. "Just the usual. Kids, dinner, bedtime routines…"

"I might be able to help you with that."

He was good with her kids, she had to hand him that. And pretty helpful with dinner prep, dishes and story time, too. She mirrored his flirtatious tone. "I'm listening."

His voice dropped another persuasive notch. "My brother Jack is hosting a potluck dinner at his place tonight. I'd like you and the kids to be my plus four."

It would definitely help not to have to cook, given that the school's Father's Day picnic was just a few days away. Aware things were starting to get a little too rowdy, she waved them in. "I'd love to but I can't. Sharon has to work until nine thirty this evening, and I told her I'd care for Shoshanna."

"You could bring her, too, if it's okay with Sharon. My

brother Jack has three girls, ages two, three and four. I think you might know them from the preschool."

Phone still to her ear, Kelly shepherded the kids back inside, to collect their backpacks and lunch sacks. "Yes, I do and they're all adorable."

"I think so, too."

The kids lined up at the water fountain in the hallway. Kelly leaned up against the wall, luxuriating in the smooth baritone of Dan's voice. It conjured up memories of all sorts of erotic things. "You're sure we wouldn't be imposing?"

"Not at all. My brother Cullen, his wife Bridgett, their baby Robby. And my sister Lulu and my brother Matt, and a couple of our close family friends, Mitzy Martin and Rio Vasquez, will all be there, too. In fact, the only family members who won't be at Jack's tonight are my brother Chase and of course my parents who are out of town."

Kelly wasn't sure whether to be happy he wanted to include her, or nervous about how things would go. She worked to keep her reply casual. "Sounds like quite a party." Too much of one?

"What can I say?" His low chuckle soothed her. "My family is big on last-minute potluck suppers. Sometimes it's the only way we can get us all—or even most of us— together. Anyway, Jack's house is plenty big enough. And I want you to meet everyone. And for them to get to know you, too."

It was a big deal, meeting the rest of the Frank and Rachel McCabe clan.

And an even bigger deal to be picked up by Dan in his brand-new eight-passenger silver SUV with gray leather interior.

"Wow, I like this!" Michael said as they moved the four booster seats into the luxurious vehicle.

Matthew and Kelly agreed. "It's so big inside!"

A bit overwhelmed, Shoshanna studied her surroundings with a shy smile.

To Kelly's joy, she and her kids and Shoshanna were welcomed as warmly by the rest of the McCabes.

And because Jack had turned the family room of his rambling abode into a giant playroom, with toys geared for preschoolers of all ages and ability, the kids were well-occupied inside. A feat that gave Kelly a moment to take everything in.

Matt, the military vet turned rancher whom she'd briefly met the night of the raccoon invasion, was definitely the strong but silent type. He also seemed to have a lot on his mind.

The widowed Jack was an attentive dad, but otherwise subdued. Mostly because he said he'd been operating on patients most of the day.

The vivacious Lulu was a real chatterbox.

Cullen and Bridgett were over the moon about the adoption of their one-year-old son, Robby, and the upcoming birth of their second child. As well as happy to see their little boy playing happily with the rest of the kids, on the family room floor. The witty, darkly handsome Rio Vasquez worked alongside Dan. But it was the beautiful and sophisticated-looking Mitzy Martin who seemed to be garnering the most attention with the "news" of her brand-new pregnancy.

Matt quirked a brow. Dan shot a look at Rio. His fellow law officer backed up, hands held high in front of him, chuckling. "Nope. I had nothing to do with this."

Gaping, Lulu turned to Mitzy. "Our brother Chase did this to you?"

Mitzy blushed fiercely at the mention of Dan's only sibling not in attendance at the impromptu get-together. "Get serious!" she said. "That is never going to happen."

Lulu made a whimsical face. "That's what the two of you said before you got together the first time!"

Oh dear, Kelly thought as an awkward silence fell.

Dan turned to Kelly, explaining, "Mitzy and Chase were briefly engaged before they broke it off."

"And that was years ago," Mitzy interjected firmly, looking as if she had come to terms with whatever heart-break had transpired between her and Dan's brother Chase. "So how about we celebrate my decision to go it alone via fertility treatments and AI and go on from there!" she suggested, her excitement contagious.

They toasted to Bridgett's and Mitzy's pregnancies, and then, aware the kids had to be getting hungry, began assembling the potluck buffet. They were nearly finished setting everything out when Michelle appeared at Kelly's side. "Mommy?" she said plaintively, looking like she was going to cry. Her lower lip thrust out. "Shoshanna's sad again."

"Mitzy was really good with Shoshanna tonight," Kelly told Dan hours later. The exhausted triplets were upstairs, sound asleep in their beds. In no hurry to end the evening, they'd retreated to her backyard patio. She'd set a hurricane lantern on the picnic table to their left, and it lit the area with a cozy glow.

"So were you and Lulu." Dan opened the bottle of chilled white wine that she'd had in her fridge for just such an occasion.

Kelly set two glasses on the table. "Actually, everyone chipped in to get the playtime back on track." Noting how good he looked this evening, in jeans and an untucked pale blue button-up, her gaze drifted upward to admire his dark rumpled hair and the hint of evening beard on his face. She sighed appreciatively. This man was truly the epitome of masculine sexiness.

A thrill sweeping through her, she continued, "Still, it was Mitzy who suggested we call the dealership and get Sharon on the phone for a few minutes."

Once the three-year-old had FaceTimed with her mom, and was reassured that although both mother and daughter would be arriving home later than usual, Sharon would be there to read her stories and tuck her in, Shoshanna had calmed down and been fine the rest of the evening.

Dan handed her the bottle and Kelly poured wine into two goblets. "No doubt about it, Mitzy is going to be a great mom."

Dan nodded agreeably as they settled onto the cushioned glider with their wine. "Mitzy has always been great with kids."

Kelly snuggled into the curve of his body. Asked curiously, "What does she do, anyway?"

Briefly, Dan paused. And for a second, Kelly had the distinct impression he didn't want to tell her. Finally, he said, "She works for the Laramie County Department of Child and Family Services."

Kelly froze. She swiveled to face him, her shoulder bumping his. "You're not joking."

With a shrug, he draped his arm along the back of the glider. "She's the best social worker they have."

So many memories came flooding back to Kelly. Very few of them anywhere near pleasant. Anxiety warred with the sharp sensation of betrayal. Before she knew it, she was on her feet, setting her glass of wine aside.

"Was tonight some sort of trap? To get me to change my mind about social workers?"

Shaking his head, Dan rolled to his feet, too. He set his glass next to hers.

"It was pure circumstance." He paused to let his words sink in. "Jack invited Lulu and Rio, and they both really wanted Mitzy to come, too."

Kelly had to admit that she had noticed a real closeness and camaraderie between Rio and Mitzy and Dan's siblings.

She swallowed and, aware she may have overreacted, sat back down on the glider. "What's going on with her?"

Dan retrieved their glasses and joined her. He sat close, his body warm and comforting. "Grief, mostly. Although I've heard she and her Dallas socialite mother do not get along that well. Anyway, Mitzy's been struggling since her dad died a few months ago, and this is her first Father's Day without him."

"Is that why she decided to get pregnant now?"

"I think that's been in the works for a while. In any case, none of us knew she was pregnant. Although I doubt she would have announced it had Chase been there tonight." He sipped his wine, and draped a hand along the back of the glider before turning his attention to the brilliant half-moon and abundant stars overhead. "Those two still walk on eggshells around each other."

Reassured, Kelly settled back into the curve of his body. "Do you think Chase and Mitzy will ever get back together?"

Dan shrugged and regarded her in a way that left no doubt they would be making love again, very soon. "All I can tell you is that after growing up with our mom and dad's marriage as an example, all of us kids have set a very high bar for our relationships. We all want what they still have. A deep enduring love that will handle whatever is thrown our way."

Recalling the tenderness of his touch, Kelly sipped her wine. "You don't think Chase can get that with Mitzy?"

He finished his drink, leaned over to set the glass aside, then sat back and rested his arm around her shoulders. "Depends on if they are willing to change. Right now they seem to be opposites in nearly every way."

Kelly paused to reflect. "In any case, Mitzy seemed nice."

Brow furrowing, he slanted her a glance. "Unlike most of the social workers you've known?"

Kelly finished her own glass of wine and set it down. "As you know," she retorted lightly, swinging back around to face him, "I'm not a fan of bureaucracy of any kind."

"I got that." He shifted her onto his lap and leaned in flirtatiously. "But I hear some deputies are okay."

She chuckled at his exaggerated drawl, loving the playful turn their encounter was taking.

She rested her index finger on her chin and pretended to think. Finally allowing, "You're right. Rio Vasquez is kind of cute."

Dan burst out laughing.

"Shh!" She snuggled closer. "You'll wake up the kids."

Her mock scolding tone had him sitting up straighter, an action that nicely delineated the warm, hard muscles in his masculine physique. He scored his thumb across her lips. "We don't want that."

A melting sensation started deep inside her. "No." Kelly shifted even more intimately on his lap. "We don't." The kiss he delivered was slow and hot. She arched against him, feeling his demanding hardness.

He stroked a hand through her hair. "So, you had a good time at Jack's tonight?"

They kissed again, and she savored the feel of his lips on hers. "I did."

He worked his way down her throat. Dropping butterfly kisses and caresses. "All those McCabes, all those kids, weren't too much for you?"

Lord, he felt good, she thought, as she gazed into his eyes and ran her hands across the width of his broad, strong shoulders. "No. I've always wanted to be part of a big, extended family." Smiling, went on to admit, "Always wanted to have five or six kids."

"Well, what do you know?" He ran a hand down her thigh. "I just happen to have recently purchased a seven-bedroom home in the country with plenty of room for kids to play."

"Not to mention an eight-passenger vehicle that's both comfy and safe as can be."

He kissed her again. Once. And then again and again. Finally, she lifted her head and said breathlessly, "Dan?"

"Hmm?" He sighed, looking every bit as besotted as she felt. "I'm glad you invited me to go with you this evening. Tonight was just what I needed."

"Me, too," he said, serious now.

Heart skittering in her chest, Kelly found herself doing what really interested men did before an evening's end—nail down the next date!

Not that she and Dan were dating…exactly. But she was surprised to find she'd actually like to be. She moistened her lips. Gathered her courage and plunged on. "Which brings us to our next dilemma."

Still holding her eyes, he brought her hand to his mouth and kissed her knuckles. Prompting an all-over quiver.

"And what's that?" His voice was a sexy rumble in his chest.

"What are you doing tomorrow night?" she ventured shyly.

"I don't know yet." Teasingly, he waggled his brows. "Maybe the better question to ask is what are *you* doing tomorrow night?"

She flushed. "Last-minute prep for the preschool picnic Saturday evening."

"Ah. I'm guessing you might need help with that."

"Actually," Kelly stated, tilting her head to one side, "now that you mention it, your assistance would be very much appreciated." So much so she could easily see herself beginning to depend on him.

"Good," he said, taking advantage of the proximity and kissing her again, slowly and thoroughly, before pausing to look deep into her eyes. "Because I have to tell you, sweetheart, there is nowhere else I'd rather be than right here with you."

Chapter Twelve

"Come on in, Deputy Dan!" Michelle said the following evening, opening the door wide. "We're making cookies and cupcakes for decorating at the summer picnic!"

He followed her through the living room toward the kitchen, where Kelly stood in front of the whirring mixer. Her cheeks were flushed a pretty pink, and her hair was swept up in a clip on the back of her head.

Dan caught her glance, smiling at the captivating image she made, then turned back to the child giving him the tour. "Are they in the oven now?"

"Yes. Well—" Michelle wrinkled her nose, in that moment looking very much like her gorgeous mom "—some of them are!" She sighed loudly.

Michael came over to say hello to Dan, via their traditional hands slaps of high and low fives. He chimed in, "Mommy says we have to bake *bunches* more. But we can't stay up till they are all done."

Matthew greeted Dan, too. Then peered at him closely. "What 'bout you, Deputy Dan? Can you stay up until they are done?"

"I hope so. But I don't know. I might get—" Dan paused to tickle them all "—sleepy!"

Wild giggles followed.

They tickled him back.

With an exasperated shake of her head, Kelly came around the kitchen island. She propped her hands on her hips. Then gave him the look he was beginning to know so well. The one that said she wanted to kiss him—but wouldn't—as long as their talkative audience was in residence.

She feigned a sternness that no one took seriously. "Okay, my little helpers, let's get back to work."

The kids returned to their various stations at the island. Standing on the step stool with her name on it, Michelle announced, "We're filling the cupcake tins! Want to help?"

"Of course!" Dan stepped in. "So what flavors are these cupcakes going to be?" he asked as if he didn't know.

Michael puffed out his chest importantly. "Vanilla."

Matthew nodded emphatically. "Mommy says they have to be *all vanilla* 'cause some kids can't have *chocolate* before bed."

Dan nodded solemnly. "I can see where it might keep some people awake." Like naughty dreams and wicked fantasies of the woman opposite him were keeping him awake.

"Plus," Kelly added, gliding over to stand next to him, infusing him with her sweet feminine scent, which only made him want to kiss her all the more. As if she could read his thoughts, she moved her knee slightly, nudging it against the uppermost curve of his calf. A sensual warmth infused him.

Hints of a few stolen kisses yet to come?

He could only hope so.

Although he found hanging out with her and the kids pretty damn satisfying, too.

Oblivious to the depths of his yearnings, she continued, explaining the reasons behind the selection. "Vanilla is white, and white will make the colored sprinkles prettier in the end."

"I see."

They continued the baking marathon for another half hour. Dan couldn't say who enjoyed themselves more, him or the kids. He only knew that Kelly looked as happy and content as he felt.

But that, like all good things, had to come to an end.

When the clock reached eight, Kelly told the triplets, "It's time to get ready for bed."

"Can I be of assistance in any way?" Dan asked, looking at the empty mixing bowls and utensils scattered around the kitchen. He might not be that much of a cook, but he did know how to do the dishes.

"What's 'ssistance?" Matthew handed Kelly his batter-splattered apron.

"Help," Michael said, giving up his apron, "and Mommy doesn't need any. She can do things *all by herself.*"

Although Dan was sure that was true, she shouldn't have to. She should have a man beside her, helping her raise her delightful family. And that man should be him.

His glance held Kelly's as he waited for her to decide. He wasn't surprised to see she seemed uncertain about how much to include him.

He was uncertain how hard and far to push.

Even though he knew what he wanted. All of them together, all of the time.

Finally, whatever inner battle she'd been having over, she smiled. "Actually, I could use a hand tonight." Her eyes held his an intimately long moment. Gratitude and something else he couldn't quite identify was reflected on her face. "Would you mind taking the kids into the living room and reading them a few bedtime stories while I run their bathwater and get their jammies laid out for them?"

Glad to be of service, wishing he could do more, Dan smiled at her and said, "No problem."

I HOPE I DON'T live to regret this, Kelly thought, as she headed upstairs. Because at this time of night her over-tired triplets had only one volume.

Excruciatingly loud.

Hence, no matter where she was on the second floor, she could hear every word being said. And so far there weren't many stories being read.

"We miss the goats, Deputy Dan," Michelle noted plaintively. "Can we see their pictures?"

Dan's low sexy voice rumbled, "You certainly can."

There was another long pause as Kelly got towels out of the linen closet and stacked them on the bathroom counter. "Is that their new home?" Michael asked.

"Yes."

"They look happy," Michelle said.

"They are," Dan reassured her, and his inherent kindness and patience made Kelly smile.

She ventured a look over the bannister and saw all three kids nestled on and around Dan, just as they would have done had he actually been their daddy.

A sentimental knot formed in her throat. If only he had been, how different all their lives would have been!

"Do you think they miss us?" Matthew asked, resting his head on Dan's broad shoulder.

Dan put his cell phone aside and hugged all three of them close simultaneously. "I'm sure they do, but they have other new friends, too."

A brief silence fell as the kids considered that.

Kelly went to check on the tub and found the water needed a little more bubble bath.

"Are they ever going to get married?" Michelle wanted to know. "Because they are girl goats, you know."

Good question, Kelly thought, trying not to chuckle. She hazarded another peek. From what she could see of the lawman's profile, he had an amazingly straight face.

Dan paused. Finally, he said, "Goats don't really get married."

"How come?" Matthew asked, inquisitive as ever.

Dan paused. "I don't really know."

Kelly went to turn down their beds.

"Mommy wants to get married," Michelle said.

Oh, no...no!

Kelly rushed back toward the stairs. Too late. Dan was already fighting a chuckle. "Really? Because I've never heard her say that."

Mortified, Kelly covered her face with her hands. Why had she ever thought leaving the talkative triplets alone with the man she was hopelessly attracted to was a good idea? Even for a single second?

"That's because she doesn't want to get married," Michael interrupted fiercely, independent as ever.

"Yes, she does," Michelle argued back stubbornly. "And anyways, she won't be happy till she is married."

Two weeks ago Kelly would have said that absolutely was not true. She was deliriously content being the single mom of three. But that was before Dan had come into her life, bringing with him an excitement and a tenderness that she had never before experienced.

He'd made her realize she was still a flesh and blood woman, with needs that had long gone unmet. He'd made her realize that despite the many friends she had made in Laramie, she still had an inner loneliness only he could ease.

He'd made her realize she didn't necessarily want to continue on this path alone.

That she might want a man beside her.

A husband, even.

She might want *him*.

Down below, the conversation continued.

"You want to know what I think?" Dan said, his low voice rumbling in that wonderful way of his when he wanted to get them back on track.

"Yes!" two out of three said.

Kelly ventured what she promised herself would be one last peek. Saw Dan regard all three of her children solemnly, even as he took the time to look each and every one of them in the eye. "I think the only thing your mom needs to be happy is to know that the three of you love her as much as she loves you, which is a whole lot, don't you think?"

Kelly smiled. Good save, Deputy Dan, good save! What a land mine he had just sidestepped.

"Yes," the triplets chorused. "Mommy loves us as much as the entire world, as big as the sky, even as much as vanilla ice cream!"

"Well, that is a lot," Dan agreed.

Kelly couldn't help but grin, but then sobered a bit as she realized he had deftly dodged the whole idea of her getting married. To him or to, well, anyone. Was that a good or bad sign, considering how often she had proclaimed that she had no wish whatsoever to ever get married again? Whereas he had proclaimed his own desire to get married. And settle down. Theoretically speaking, anyway...

"And you know what else she loves, Deputy Dan?" Michelle finished with an emphatic statement that quickly had Kelly groaning and bracing herself. "You!"

Kelly used that moment to rather noisily head down the stairs. "Kids, bath time! Now!"

They groaned and carried on, but finally went upstairs with her to do her bidding. Luckily, they were so tired from their very busy day that they fell asleep the minute their heads hit the pillows. The final childcare chore of the day completed, Kelly headed back down the stairs.

Her kitchen was remarkably tidy, considering the state she had left it in, and Dan was at the sink, elbow deep in sudsy water, finishing up.

"You didn't have to do all this!"

He turned to her. "I told you I wanted to help."

She nodded.

Silence stretched between them.

She figured if someone had to talk about the elephant in the room, it might as well be her. Swallowing, she grabbed a dish towel and closed the distance between them. "Sorry about the matchmaking."

He waggled his brows at her. Seeming to wonder why she was in such a tizzy. "They're cute."

As was he.

Too cute to let get away.

Never mind be chased away by her oft overexuberant triplets. She drew a deep breath. "They are cute. And constantly questioning. And independent, to a fault sometimes. Not to mention over the top romantic!"

"So?" Finished, he dried his hands, then placed them about her waist, guiding her close. He looked down at her affectionately. "I love all of it."

But would he continue to do so? Kelly wondered, her knees shaking and her heart pounding. How would she feel if he didn't? And why was she suddenly so anxious about everything? Feeling as though absolutely everything was on the line?

Aware he was studying her closely, she drew a breath. Attempted to pull herself together. "I wish I could say they'll stop pestering you about the goats soon, but…"

He tucked a hand beneath her chin. His eyes were dark, shuttering. Mouth lowering, he whispered, "The heart wants what the heart wants."

And what hers wanted, Kelly thought, as he kissed her, slowly and thoroughly, and she kissed him back, just as passionately, was this man and this moment in time. She wanted him in her life, in her home, in her bed. But how to achieve that with three tiny chaperones, constantly underfoot, was yet something else she was just going to have to figure out…

In the meantime, she still needed help getting ready for the picnic. So… Hopefully, she asked, "Are you busy tomorrow evening?"

He leaned closer, his manner as kind as it was self-assured. His warm breath whispered across her temple. "Whatever you need, sweetheart." He kissed her again, slowly and seductively. Then promised, "I'm here."

DAN ARRIVED ON Kelly's doorstep at six o'clock Friday evening, just as the pizza delivery man was leaving. Flashing her a lazy grin and sporting a day's worth of stubble on his jaw, he was the picture of rugged masculinity. She felt her heart give a little jolt. Why did he have to be so darn attractive? And why couldn't she stop wanting to make love with him when she knew it made her more emotionally vulnerable?

"I heard the kids are at my brother Jack's house for the evening."

Talk about providence, Kelly thought, happy about the unexpected turn of events. Casually, she ushered him into the breakfast nook, where two places had already been set at the table.

She moved the piping hot pizza onto a serving platter, then gestured for him to help himself, as they sat down. "Your sister Lulu called this morning. She said she was hosting a kiddie movie night with her three nieces at Jack's this evening, and the girls wanted the triplets to come, too. I was all too glad to RSVP yes on their behalf since I have yet to put together the bags for the beanbag toss."

He grinned as they started to eat. "Ah, so that's why you invited me to come over."

It was certainly one reason. Albeit not the most important one. She spared him a flirtatious glance. "Is that awful of me?"

He spared her one back. "Not at all." His voice dropped to a tantalizing rumble. "As I said, I'm happy to help out in whatever way I can."

A fact that made him all the more desirable, Kelly noted with a wistful sigh.

They chatted amiably while they finished eating, then cleared the space and set up shop in the breakfast room.

They spent the next fifteen minutes cutting out squares of fabrics. Then, while Kelly sewed them into open-ended bags, he measured out dry white beans and filled each.

"You're pretty handy with that sewing machine," Dan noted in open admiration as she swiftly sewed the filled bags closed.

He brought her a few more, and Kelly inadvertently caught another whiff of his masculine scent. "All I am doing is sewing straight seams."

"Still," he noted, his face filled with purpose, as he

came close enough to gather up the finished bags and hand her a new crop to finish off, "they're straight."

She loved the fact he took anything related to the kids' happiness so seriously. Aware this was the kind of thing they'd be doing, if they were married, she said, "You expected them to be crooked?"

He chuckled at her light, playful tone. Then, frustrated with all the getting up and down, scooted his chair closer to hers to make the hand off. So close in fact their knees were now touching. He didn't move away, and neither did she. "Mine would be."

Aware of the body-to body heat, she swallowed. Then pushed aside her yearning long enough to bat her lashes at him and quip, "Don't sell yourself short, Deputy. You're measuring out the dry beans and filling these little bags up like a pro."

He squinted at her affectionately. "How many of these did you say we had to do?"

She tried not to think how intimate it felt, sitting here together, sharing the school-related task. "We've got five cloth targets, so I wanted to make about fifty." So far, they'd only done ten.

To his credit, he did not complain. He simply got busier. As did she. "Have you always known how to sew?"

"I learned in college. I got a job at a fabric store to help me pay my way through." She paused to rethread the bobbin on the machine. "To move up from half to full time, I had to learn to sew. Monogram. Use a pattern."

Deciding he might be as thirsty as she was, she got up and poured them both tall glasses of raspberry lemonade. Their fingers brushed as she handed him his.

Another jolt of desire went through her.

Wishing they weren't in such a time crunch, she watched him take a deep drink.

"You didn't want to do it for a profession?"

"No." Kelly drenched her dry throat, then went back to sewing. "I always knew I wanted to work with kids. Preferably, those under five."

"How come?" He studied her curiously.

Kelly bent her head, fighting the continuing flush of awareness. "They seemed the most vulnerable." She met his eyes candidly. "I knew a good experience could shape how young children felt about school from then on, so I wanted it to be positive. Create a safe, nurturing space."

Admiration shone in his eyes. "You've done that. With your own kids. And from what I could see, those in your preschool class, too."

Warming at his praise, Kelly sighed and shook her head. "I still miss things, though."

His dark brows knit. "Like what?"

Kelly pursed her lips. "Shoshanna last night." Regretfully, she admitted, "I should have put together the fact that her dad died less than a year ago. They've moved to a new place, and she is in a new school. And her mom has recently been sick with the stomach flu. She's three and a half years old! It's no wonder she's worried and having major separation anxiety."

Dan nodded sympathetically. "Has she said anything more to you about the 'little man'?"

That was a puzzle. "No. But this morning in class she did say her mom cried when she woke up and tried to get out of bed." The offhand comment had stayed with Kelly all day.

Dan paused. "You think that's a manifestation of grief?"

Their eyes met, held. "Could be." Kelly bit her lower lip. "I know I felt that way a lot of days after my divorce. And again, with it being Father's Day—their first without

Shoshanna's daddy—I imagine it's pretty heart-wrenching for both of them." The last bag sewn shut, Kelly stood and stretched.

Dan got to his feet, too. "Shoshanna and Sharon are lucky to have you in their lives."

Kelly stepped away from the table. "Thank you for saying that." *Thank you for so many things...*

DAN DIDN'T KNOW how much time they had left before they had to pick up Kelly's kids. He did know he didn't want to waste a single second of it.

He caught her hand and reeled her in close until he was inundated with the sweet softness of her once again. She was stunning any time of day or night, but she had never looked more radiant than she did at that moment. More womanly or full of need.

Heart racing, he lifted a hand and undid the clasp in her hair, which fell in silky untamed waves, framing her beautiful face, teasing her slender shoulders. "Dan..." she whispered tremulously, lifting her eyes up to his.

He let his gaze drift over her. Loving the way she looked back at him, with a purity and innocence that rocked him to his core. "You are so damn beautiful," he growled, pausing to kiss her with all the pent-up emotion he had. "So damn sexy."

Wreathing her arms about his neck, she kissed him back with sweet deliberation. "Right back at you, cowboy..." Lips still surrendering to his, she let her hands drift across the width of his shoulders, down his spine, over his hips.

"So..." Feeling her melt against him, he kissed her cheek, her temple, the delicate skin behind her ear. "Is that a yes we can make love, or a no we can't?"

The feisty look in her eyes invited him to run wild with her. She slanted her head to one side. Began unbuttoning his shirt, even as she inundated him with another kiss that was soft and sexy and achingly sweet. "What do you think?" she whispered as she spread her questing fingertips across his chest.

That I would be lost without you. But not sure she was ready to hear that just yet, he merely smiled and shifted her more fully against him. "That you want me as much as I want you."

Trembling now, she rocked seductively against his hardness. "Maybe more…"

Not possible. Victory in store, he chuckled. "We'll see about that." His body aching with the need to possess her, he bent his head and kissed her in the all-consuming way he had been longing to kiss her all evening. Determined to make her see what they could have if she would just let him all the way into her heart, he deepened the kiss even more. Then all pretense that this was nothing more than a reckless affair ended. She met him kiss for kiss. Desire thundering through him in waves, he flattened the hard length of his body against the soft pliability of hers. Able to feel how much Kelly wanted and needed him, no matter what she said, he swept her mouth with his tongue, kissing her hotly until she gave him everything he had ever desired, everything he needed. Before long, the blood was pooling hot and urgent in his body, and he wanted her more than he had ever imagined he could.

When Kelly sagged against him, signaling that she felt the same sizzling intensity, he broke off the embrace just long enough to slip an arm beneath her knees and lift her against his chest.

"Bedroom?" she said.

He was all for being comfortable, too. "You bet." Grinning, he carried her up the stairs and down the hall to the frilly covers on her bed. The need to make her his—not just for tonight, but forever—was stronger than ever.

Gently, he set her down.

Once again, their lips met in a searing connection of want and need.

Wonder swept through Kelly, along with the knowledge that this chemistry they felt, the connection they'd discovered, was something to be treasured.

So what if there were no guarantees where any of this would lead, she thought as his hands eased beneath her T-shirt and caressed her breasts. He kissed and touched her as if he never wanted to see their mutual affection end. And the truth was, neither did she.

Drawing the knit top over her head, he divested her of her bra. He guided her backward, her weight braced against his arm, then kissed his way from her lips, to her throat to the curves of her breasts and the valley between. Her skin heated. Desire ran riot inside her. "I want you naked," he murmured, rubbing his thumbs across her taut nipples, cupping the weight in his hands.

She watched as if in a languid dream as his lips closed over the aching crowns. Suckled gently.

"Dan…"

"We're not hurrying, sweetheart. Not this time…"

Claiming her lips again, he unzipped her shorts and eased his hand beneath the waistband of her panties. Tenderly caressed her stomach, then moved lower. She gasped, aware she had never felt this beautiful, sensual. Ready.

His lips met hers and he kissed her lovingly, as if this chance might never come again. Silken brushes of his fingertips alternated with the sensual rubbing of his palm.

Her knees weakened.

Before she knew it, she was freefalling over the edge,

coming apart in his arms. His breath hot and rough against her throat, he held her until her quaking stopped, then finished undressing her, and a short minute later joined her, naked, on the bed.

Indulging in her most secret fantasies, Kelly took her time exploring the sinew and heat of his strong, masculine body. Her hair falling across his chest, she kissed her way down the treasure trail, found him velvety hot and hard.

Over and over, she kissed and caressed, teasing and tempting, loving and adoring, until he too could stand it no more.

Together, they rolled on the condom.

He sat against the headboard and took her with him, lifting her ever so gently and carefully onto his lap. They kissed again, ravenously, until all that seemed to matter to either of them was the desire sweeping through them in waves.

His hands cupped her hips as she shifted and made them one. Moving in a slow, sensual rhythm, they merged their bodies as intimately as they had already begun to merge their lives. Together, they found new heights…until there was nothing but the all-consuming, ever-expanding feelings flowing freely between them…nothing but this wild yearning…this incredible passion…this sweet-hot connection…and this moment in time.

HARD TO IMAGINE that this could be his favorite time with Kelly, Dan mused, as she collapsed against his chest, sated and completely out of breath. But, as he cuddled her against him, reveling in her still-heated skin and feminine vulnerability, he knew it was. Maybe because the only time she stopped expecting to be inevitably hurt, betrayed or abandoned, and truly let her guard down with him, was when they made love and snuggled together after.

So he held her, savoring the closeness, the intimacy, until he felt her stiffen ever so slightly, heard her wistful sigh, and knew they were headed back to normality again.

He stroked her hair, wishing he could keep her in that dream state a little longer.

Long enough to trust him.

Want a life with him.

Another sigh.

He found his muscles tensing, too. "What?" he whispered in her ear.

Lithely, she disengaged their bodies and rose, reaching for her discarded undies. "I was just wishing we could stay and play—" she flashed a come-hither smile "—a little longer, but I've got to pick up the kids from Jack's house."

Ah, the demands of real life. He shrugged and, aware that duty called, rose reluctantly, too. "I could call my brother…" Jack had had the love of his life once. When he'd been with his late wife. He would understand.

Lulu yearned for the same.

Hell, all his sibs did. Maybe because their parents had such an incredible marital partnership.

Kelly slipped on her bra and panties. "And tell him and Lulu what?" Swiftly, she tugged on her T-shirt, then her shorts. "That we can't come and get the triplets yet because we're too busy making love?"

He grinned as the possibility took root. "It's an idea."

For a moment, she looked tempted. Then regret shimmered through her. "No," she said with a soft, almost disappointed sigh, "it's already late. They need to get their baths and go to bed soon."

Finished dressing, Dan folded his arms about her in a hug. "Rain check then?"

She returned his tender glance in a way that led him to believe that although they might not be there yet, they absolutely were on a path to something every bit as wonderful and long-lasting as his folks still had. She rose on tiptoe to give him a quick, hopeful kiss. "A definite rain check," she vowed.

TEN MINUTES LATER, they were headed for the door when Dan's cell phone let out a distinctive beep. He looked at the screen. "Sorry. I have to take this." He put the phone to his ear. Listened intently, then said gruffly, "No. I'll handle it. I'm headed there now."

Concerned, Kelly asked, "What's up?"

Dan exhaled. "I put an alert in the daily briefing a few days ago, asking other officers to keep an eye on Sharon Johnson's residence on West Elm. To let me know if they saw anything unusual."

Hardly able to believe he'd put what Shoshanna said to her in confidence, at school, in the official police record, Kelly gaped at him. "Has something happened?" She didn't know whether to feel angry or betrayed. Maybe a little of both.

Dan pocketed his phone, as calm as she was not. His features were rigid with tension. "The patrolling officer on duty tonight isn't sure. He says there is a Mercedes with Houston plates parked out in front of the Johnson home. Sharon's on the porch with a man he presumes to be the driver of the vehicle. They seemed to be having a quiet disagreement of some sort, and she appears to be crying. She doesn't seem to be in any kind of danger. But he's staying in the vicinity, and I'm going to go over and check it out. Just in case."

Kelly followed him out the door. "Then I'm going with you!"

Dan looked ready to argue.

Swiftly, she locked the door behind them. "If Sharon's upset, she may need a woman friend."

"Fine," Dan barked, "but if I don't like the way things look when I get there, you're going to stay in the vehicle."

Kelly saw the look on his face and decided not to argue.

It took roughly three minutes to get to West Elm. Luckily, Kelly noted as they passed the patrol car halfway down the street, then parked at the edge of the property and got out of the car, little Shoshanna was nowhere in sight. The bedrooms upstairs, where she was likely sleeping, were dark and quiet.

Sharon and a tall, well-groomed man in his late forties, were seated on the cushioned glider on the front porch of her home.

While her visitor was formally dressed in a shirt and tie and dress pants, Sharon was garbed in her usual at-home attire of yoga pants and a T-shirt, sneakers. Her hair was swept up in a clip, her face bare of makeup. The ugly red butterfly rash spreading across her cheeks and nose looked even angrier than it had the other day—whether from the way she was crying or because her menopause-related skin condition was getting worse, Kelly didn't know. What she did hear was Sharon saying a very definitive "No!" as she shook her head at the unidentified man opposite her.

Dan took the sidewalk to her home with long purposeful strides, his manner calm and coolly authoritative. Kelly was right beside him. "Everything okay?" he asked.

Sharon jumped, startled to realize they had an audience.

"Yes." She sniffed and stood, wringing her hands in front of her. "This is Bart Little, a physician-friend of my late husband." She paused. "He was just leaving."

With a reluctant grimace, Dr. Little stood.

Dan looked from one to the other. It was clear, Kelly noted, there was still a lot of tension remaining. "You're sure everything is okay?" Dan persisted.

"No," Bart Little snapped, swinging around and looking Dan and Kelly right in the eye. "And it won't be until someone can talk sense into Sharon." Bart turned back to her and said with a beleaguered sigh, "You know where to reach me if you change your mind."

Sharon said nothing in response.

Silence reigned as Bart Little retraced his steps, got in his car and drove away.

Seeming, belatedly, to realize they deserved some kind of explanation, Sharon turned to them and offered lamely, "I never should have called Bart and told him that—" She stopped abruptly, as if censoring herself, swallowed and tried again. "Bottom line. He thinks the only way Shoshanna and I will be happy is if we move back to Houston and lean on all our old friends there."

That sort of made sense, Kelly thought. Sharon had been under a lot of stress in her new job at the dealership, and—in the absence of any extended family she could lean on—was still in the process of building a support system for her and her child here in Laramie. But Kelly didn't know what kind of support system Sharon really had in Houston, either. If it had been great, wouldn't Sharon have stayed? Instead of moving here? She studied her friend. "You don't want that?"

Again, Sharon hesitated. Finally, she said, "No. Not that I blame Bart for his concern, even if it is misguided. He thinks he is doing and saying what my late husband would have wanted. But life in the big city is not what either Shoshanna or I need right now. So, Bart and everyone else we left behind is just going to have to accept that. And stop calling me and texting me and emailing me. Because all it's doing is upsetting me! And to be honest, Shoshanna, too."

"Well, at least we know what Shoshanna was talking about when she said 'the little man' made her mommy cry," Kelly said after they'd apologized for interrupting what should have been a private moment. They said goodbye to Sharon and walked back to Dan's SUV.

He was quiet as they climbed in. Kelly turned to him. "You think there's more going on than what Sharon said though, don't you?"

Dan shot her a grim smile. The knowledge gleaned from years of working in law enforcement was reflected in his eyes. "There always is." He clasped her hand in his. "But right now we have your kids to pick up and a summer picnic to get ready for tomorrow." He lifted her wrist to his lips, kissed the inside until her insides went warm and liquid. "So why don't we just concentrate on that?"

Chapter Thirteen

"The kids aren't with you?" Dan noted the next morning when he met her over at the preschool, bright and early. He was wearing a T-shirt and jeans, and looked sexy as all get-out. He smelled good, too, like sandalwood and soap.

Kelly grabbed two flatbed carts and walked with him away from the hub of activity, where other parents were already busy helping to set up the big white dining tent on the lawn, toward the parking lot.

Aware how easily they moved together, no matter what they were doing, she smiled and met his eyes. "There's no way I could keep an eye on them, so I made a deal with the other three-year-old-class teacher, Cece Taylor. I'd do all her work here if she watched the triplets."

He flashed a warm smile, similar to the one he gave her when he was about to make love to her. "It won't be too much for Cece?"

Telling herself this was not the time or place to indulge in tantalizing fantasies, Kelly replied in her most matter-of-fact tone, "She has two teenagers at home who've offered to help. Plus, the kids know her from school and adore her. So, no, it won't be too much. And it will save Cece being out in the June heat all day."

They paused next to his SUV, with the attached trailer. "So it's a win-win."

"Sounds like." Dan opened up the back of the trailer. Together, they lifted out the Go Fishing game tables, cloth targets and bags for the beanbag toss, and stacked them onto the first cart.

Finished, Dan asked, "Where do you want me to unload the folding tables and chairs?"

Kelly helped him lift out the first long table. Out of the corner of her eye, she saw her nemesis approaching her and girded herself for battle. "Well, here comes Mirabelle now. Let's ask her."

The power mom slammed to a halt in front of them, temper flaring. "I can't believe you're really doing this!"

Kelly looked the other woman in the eye. "Really? Because I recall you telling me if the single parents and their children wanted to sit together in groups that I was going to have to supply the tables. And, thanks to the generosity of Dan's parents, I have."

Mirabelle glared. "You're going to ruin the ambience."

Dan started to intervene, but Kelly curved a staying hand over his forearm, wordlessly letting him know she could and would handle this. She turned back to the parent who had caused her and others so much grief. "I don't see how," she said calmly.

Mirabelle gave a dismissive sniff. "This is supposed to be a Father's Day celebration, not a run-of-the-mill school carnival!"

As if this all hadn't been previously hashed out. "The director approved the additional games."

"She also told you that you had to work *with me* and the other mothers on the parent committee."

Unfortunately, that was all too true. And instead, Kelly had been mostly avoiding them, and the conflict that always followed, hoping if she saved any further contretemps for today that the brouhaha would be short-lived.

A strategy, she saw now, that was probably a mistake.

Mirabelle leaned in, nostrils flaring. "Of course, I get why you don't understand the importance of a day like today, Kelly. Your kids never even had a father!" she huffed indignantly. "At least until Dan McCabe stepped in to fill the void."

Nice. Kelly didn't dare turn to see what Dan was thinking or feeling. At that particular moment, she wasn't sure she wanted to know. Especially since he had never even come close to saying he loved her. Yes, they were sleeping together in a no-strings-attached way. And had fun together. He cared for her kids, and they adored him. But he hadn't signed on to be a surrogate dad to them, even if sometimes it felt as if he had.

Nor was she even sure—despite his claim to want a large and loving family of his own one day—that he was ready to take on such a huge responsibility.

At least not permanently.

Thrown off guard by the jab about an increasingly intimate relationship she wasn't the least bit ready to take public, she protested, more quietly than ever, "He isn't..."

"Oh, please!" Mirabelle tossed her head. "Save the denials for someone who will believe it!" The woman's harsh words rang in the silence that fell. Other parents had moved closer to see what the ruckus was all about.

Kelly was shocked to see that no one else looked stunned by the revelation. Did everyone know how she was beginning to feel about Dan? It appeared so.

Kelly turned slightly to her left, able to see Dan watching her with his customary law-enforcement cool. He hadn't said a word to Mirabelle because she'd silently pleaded with him not to, yet he was still here, steady and warm and waiting. Still supporting her, still ready to defend her if that was what she wanted.

She recalled what he'd said about small things turning into giant problems. This quarrel was about to be one, and that could ruin the day for everyone.

Still feeling his wordless encouragement, she drew a long, calming breath. Summoned up every ounce of cooperation she had. And turned back to Mirabelle. "Maybe we should talk privately," she said quietly.

Her nemesis seemed to be aware the disapproval surrounding both of them was escalating with every second that passed. "Maybe we should."

She and Mirabelle walked a good distance away from everyone else. When she was sure they couldn't be overheard, Kelly turned and looked the other woman in the eye. "I'm really not trying to ruin the event for all the kids, like yours, who are lucky enough to have fathers in their lives."

"But don't you see that's exactly what you're doing?" Mirabelle said, tears suddenly shimmering in her eyes.

Actually, Kelly didn't. "How?" she asked gently.

Mirabelle balled her fists at her sides. "By making the fathers who are here feel like it's going to be okay if they *don't* show up."

Was that what this was really all about? "Who would do that?" Kelly asked in shock.

"My husband, for one!"

Kelly knew Mirabelle's husband traveled for work all the time. "He's not coming home for Father's Day?"

"Of course he'll be home tomorrow! He's not going to disappoint our six children."

Belatedly, Kelly realized that Mirabelle's husband wasn't there now, helping with the setup for the Saturday evening summer picnic like so many of the other dads. "Is your husband going to be attending the event tonight?"

"Yes. He'll be here." Mirabelle swallowed, then continued with difficulty. "Because he thinks it's required for our preschoolers' happiness that he show up. If it's really not essential that he be here for this—if the celebration is more about summer than Father's Day—at least as far as he can see—then next year, he won't bother to come home for the school picnic." She released a quavering breath. "Which means it will be business as usual for him, with him hundreds of miles away at one of his many party supply businesses across the state. And I'll be here alone with the kids, just like everyone else who's not married, and it's not fair!"

"No, that's not fair," Kelly empathized quietly. Especially for the woman who—at least in terms of money and success—had everything. It was her husband's attention to and devotion to her and their kids that was lacking. No wonder Mirabelle was so insecure. She was holding on so tightly to everything she had because she was afraid of losing it. "But I don't think your husband or any of the other dads are going to see much of anything but the work you have put in to make this evening so special for them.

"They're not going to worry about what anyone else is doing or not doing. They're going to be focused on their own families. And it's my hope that the kids—like mine—who aren't as lucky as yours will be so busy having a good time, too, that they won't be focused on what they don't have."

Silence fell.

"I see your point," Mirabelle said finally, abruptly looking every bit as emotionally exhausted as Kelly felt.

"So maybe we can work together instead of against each other?" Kelly prompted. "And do our best to make the picnic this evening a roaring success?"

Her slender shoulders slumping with relief, Mirabelle smiled. "I'd like that."

They spent the next twenty minutes discussing how to best set up the extra games, and seating, then Kelly went back to Dan. He leveled an assessing gaze on her. "Everything okay?"

"Yes." Although she and Mirabelle would probably never be friends, they had finally come to an understanding. And she owed him for that.

For the next six hours, Dan and Kelly worked tirelessly along with all the other parent volunteers. At three o'clock, with the temperature inching past the one hundred degree mark, the school grounds were finally prepared.

Dan and Kelly were sweaty, unkempt messes. "When do you pick up the kids?" he asked, walking her to her vehicle.

It was all Kelly could do not to wrap her arm about his waist and lean her head on his shoulder. "Not until five. Cece knew this was going to be grueling, so she told me to take my time. Get cleaned up first."

A sparkle appeared in his blue eyes. "Ah." A wealth of longing in that single word.

An even more potent yearning welled up inside her. She moved out of earshot of others. "What about you?"

He glanced at her affectionately. "I guess I call my brother Jack. See if he'll let me shower and change clothes at his house so I don't have to drive all the way out to my ranch and then trek back into town."

Wanting to keep the mood light and carefree, she batted her lashes at him flirtatiously. "I suppose that's one way of getting cleaned up."

Chuckling mischievously, he leaned in to whisper, "You have another?"

Warming at the sensual promise in his tone, she said, "I do."

The moment they got back to her house and walked inside, Kelly took Dan by the hand and led him upstairs.

"Good thing we're not really dating," he joked as they stripped out of their clothing and stepped into the shower in her master bath. "Otherwise who knows what might happen?"

Guilt flooded Kelly. She turned on the water, adjusting it to a nice and cozy warm, then stepped beneath the spray. "You know I was just protecting our privacy."

Trying to keep outside forces from messing with what they had.

He moved with her. Tunneling both hands through her hair and lifting her lips to his. "And you know I don't care who knows how much I want you," he said gruffly.

If Kelly hadn't, she certainly would have felt it in his kiss. She gasped as their lips forged and his mouth locked on hers in a slow, sexy caress that made her tingle from head to toe. She melted against him, her bare breasts pressed against the hardness of his chest.

He was so warm and strong. So unbelievably persistent in his pursuit of her. Rising on tiptoe, she wound her arms about his neck. Water sluicing over them, she returned his kiss. He tasted so good. So dark and male. And felt even better with his thighs and chest pressed snugly against her. She could feel the hard evidence of his desire as he slid his hands down her spine and over her hips, sliding low, cupping her against him. And still he kissed her, deeply and irrevocably, possessing her heart and soul, until she thought she would melt from the inside out.

He stepped outside the shower, then came back with the protection they needed. The next thing she knew, she was being shifted upward; her weight rested against his middle, and her legs were wrapped around his waist. The cool tile against her back, he moved up, in. Pleasure flooded her in great hot waves. And then there was no more holding back. Her eyes drifted shut, her body arched. Passion swept through her, her body shuddering and coming apart, the love she felt for him dissolving in wild, carnal waves. She whispered his name. Letting every part of her adore every part of him until at last she surrendered to a wild, untamed pleasure unlike anything she had ever known.

Chapter Fourteen

Kelly picked up her kids while Dan went off to do one last chore—get twenty bags of ice to take to the preschool. By the time he got back from his errand, she had all three kids dressed in their summer best and ready to go to the party.

"Deputy Dan!" Michelle ran up to give him a big hug. "Are you going to the picnic with us?"

Dan lifted her in his arms. "I sure am."

Matthew and Michael threw their arms around his legs and gazed up at him adoringly.

'It's going to be fun," Michael predicted.

Matthew asked, "Did you know there's going to be games and stuff to do?"

"I do. And I can't wait to play the games and decorate cookies and cupcakes with you-all."

Dan was true to his word. He even let all three kids be his "helpers" when it was his turn to man the Go Fishing game while Kelly supervised the participants in the beanbag toss. While that was going on, Sharon and Shoshanna arrived and happily made their rounds of the various activities.

They were in matching cotton dresses and sun hats. "You-all look great," Kelly said when they approached.

At least in terms of what they were wearing. Sharon was moving slowly and stiffly again.

"Thanks." Sharon smiled, looking more fatigued beneath the perfectly applied makeup than Kelly had ever seen her. She fanned herself. "It's a good thing the dinner is going to be held under the tents, though. It's really hot!"

Actually, the temperature had been dropping over the course of the last hour, with it now registering in the low nineties. Which was relatively comfortable for that time of year in West Texas. Kelly smiled. "There's cold lemonade available if you want it now."

Sharon nodded. "Maybe we will get some."

Hand in hand, they headed off in that direction.

Dan murmured in Kelly's ear. "Is she okay?"

Was Sharon a little unsteady on her feet? Or was that her imagination? Kelly kept watching and then decided maybe she was just being hypervigilant.

"Maybe she's just really tired from having a stomach virus and working so hard the past couple of weeks." At least, Kelly hoped that was all it was.

"Can we take a picture together?" Michelle asked. She pointed to the Daddy and Me photo booth and started tugging Kelly in that direction.

"Actually, I think the line is shorter in this one." Kelly led her kids toward the photo backdrop that said Laramie Preschool Summer Festival.

Matthew frowned when Dan stepped back. "Deputy Dan, you got to be in the picture!" he said.

Dan looked uncertain. Which wasn't surprising, given the way she had disclaimed their romance just hours before, claiming it to be only friendship.

The trouble was she knew now it wasn't.

And given the all-encompassing way they had just made love, so did he.

What they had was something special. And always would be. Whether or not they ever began publicly dating or said they loved each other. Or took it to the next step and eventually got married.

Which was, she realized belatedly, what she secretly wanted most of all. Dan, permanently in her life.

And apparently, so did her kids.

"Yes." Michael and Matthew jumped up and down in excitement. They tugged on his hands. "We want you to stand here with us, Deputy Dan!"

Dan looked at Kelly. Was she ready for this?

A thrill went through her, followed by a wave of tenderness and affection. Apparently, she was. They grouped together for the photo. The photographer, a local, who knew Kelly was single, asked, "Do you want to take one with just the four of you, too?"

The kids looked puzzled.

Kelly and Dan knew what he was really asking.

Did she want to remember this as the day they had all spent with Dan, or not. There was only one answer to that. Kelly smiled and reached over and squeezed his hand, this time not caring who might see, or what assumptions they might make. "No," she told the photographer happily. "We're good."

In fact, she thought, as the five of them headed beneath the tent for dinner, life had never been better. Unfortunately, the serenity did not last.

As they took their seats at the table where Sharon and Shoshanna were already sitting, things took a wrong turn. Sharon was pale and shaky. She had removed her sun hat, and along the hairline her hair was soaked with sweat. Her daughter was tense with concern.

Kelly put a hand on Sharon's shoulder and felt the heat of her friend's skin burn her fingers. "Are you okay?" It felt like she had fever.

"I'm…not sure." Abruptly, Sharon's lips turned as white as her skin.

Dan moved in, too, naturally protective and gallant as ever. Quickly, he assessed the situation. "You could have heat exhaustion," he warned.

She definitely looked like she needed to go to the ER.

Sharon started to stand. "I don't think…" Her voice trailing off; she swayed and started to collapse.

Dan and Kelly moved in tandem and caught her before she crumpled to the ground. Somehow, they were able to push her into a chair. Gasps sounded all around. Paramedics were called, as others rushed forward to help, with fellow preschool teacher Cece taking charge of not just Sharon's daughter, but Kelly's triplets, as well.

Kelly rode in the ambulance with her, while Dan followed in his Suburban. They met up again in the waiting room. Kelly felt herself welling up as she wrung her hands. "What's going to happen to Shoshanna if something happens to Sharon?" she whispered in choked voice.

For that matter, what would happen to her kids if something happened to her?

They had no one else.

She had no one.

Dan put his arms around her and held her close. His strong, male presence was like a port in the storm. "We'll work it out," he murmured, pressing a kiss in her hair and rubbing a hand reassuringly over her back.

Kelly wished she was as sure of that as he was. In any case, it was good to know she could count on him.

Especially if, as she now hoped more than ever, they had a future together.

Finally, the ER doctor, Gavin Monroe strode over to them. Concerned, he ushered Kelly and Dan into a family conference room. "Sharon is asking to leave—against medical advice."

Kelly blinked in surprise. "Why?"

Gavin exhaled. "That, you will have to get from her. Just please…do what you can to convince her to get the care she needs."

She and Dan went in.

The still alarming pale and sweaty Sharon was clad in a cotton patient gown, half sitting up in the hospital bed. She was hooked up to monitors and had an IV running in her arm.

They moved to her side. Glad for his continued support, Kelly asked her friend, "Dr. Monroe told us you're asking to leave—against medical advice. Why? What's going on?"

Sharon's anxiety rose. "I can't stay here."

Quietly, Dan interjected, "Why not?"

Sharon inhaled. "Can I trust you to keep a confidence?"

Dan and Kelly nodded in unison.

Reluctantly, she went on, "I have lupus. I was first diagnosed when my husband became ill, and I've had it for five years, although recently I was in remission. But—" she scowled "—it looks as if I'm having another flare. And if my boss finds out about it, I'll be fired."

Kelly and Dan exchanged looks. So much of what had been going on now made sense. "Is that why Bart Little came to Laramie to see you?" Kelly asked.

"Yes. He was not just my late physician-husband's friend, he was my rheumatologist. I made the mistake of contacting him and asking Bart if he'd put me back on meds until I could get back to Houston to see him. He refused."

"That's why he came to see you in person and wanted you to go back to Houston."

"Yes. Or at least be treated here."

"Why don't you want that?"

"Because if I see another rheumatologist, he'll want to do his own testing and it will end up the way it always ends up, with me in the hospital. And I can't bear to be separated from Shoshanna that way. So, I'm going to let this IV finish running, to correct the dehydration that made me faint, and then I'm going home. With or without your help!"

It was clear Sharon wasn't going to be dissuaded, at least not at that moment, so Dan and Kelly slipped out to confer.

Dan took out his phone. "I'm not supporting this lunacy and driving her home, Kelly. I'm calling social services."

Shock rolled through Kelly like a tidal wave. Trembling, she put her hand over his, stilling the motion.

Feeling like she was in the middle of a romantic comedy that had suddenly turned into a horror movie, she said, "Are you nuts? You can't do that!"

He removed her hand and stepped back. All implacable law-enforcement officer now. "Sharon has a systemic autoimmune disease."

"I know what it is, Dan," Kelly interjected impatiently. And just how challenging and heartbreaking the illness was. "My mother was a nurse."

"Then you know Sharon's immune system is attacking her own tissues and organs. That lupus is a very serious medical condition, one that can lead to all sort of complications and even death if not treated properly."

"I know that. But…" To call in social services? To-night? Instead of letting Sharon rely on her close friends while she hopefully came to her senses?

"Kelly," he said, looking at her steadily, "we don't know the extent of the damage that has already been done to her body. What we do know is that this 'flare' of hers is clearly getting worse. Dr. Monroe wants her to stay." He paused. "Someone needs to talk sense into her. Preferably someone not so emotionally close to the situation." He shrugged affably. "I think it should be Mitzy."

Kelly knew this was routine. Law enforcement always called in DCFS when they needed someone to handle the parts of a situation they were not authorized to deal with.

So she tried to cut him some slack. And talk sense into him! She folded her arms across her chest. "I agree with you that Mitzy is a very nice person."

Dan nodded. "She's worked miracles more times than I can count."

Memories of Kelly's own tumultuous childhood came flooding back.

Dread rose in the pit of her stomach.

Warily, she lifted her chin, coolly pointed out, "She also works for DCFS, Dan."

A bureaucratic organization that had ignored her own breaking heart, and fear, and done "what was best for her" time and time again.

But Dan didn't seem to care about that, as his eyes locked with hers, his determination unwavering. "Yes. She does. And they have all sorts of ways they can help her and Shoshanna."

Maybe so. They also had the power to destroy the little girl's childhood, the way Kelly's had been.

Icicles formed around her heart. She stared at Dan, reminding, "DCFS can also declare Sharon temporarily unable to care for her daughter and put Shoshanna in foster care for days and weeks and even months on end!"

Dan stepped closer, his arms outstretched. "That's not going to happen here in Laramie County, Kelly, not under these circumstances. Not if there are other options, and I promise you, there will be."

She stepped away from the offered comfort of his warm embrace. Her spine stiff, she turned away. "You don't know that," she choked out.

He moved so she had no choice but to look at him. "Yes, Kelly, I do."

Tears misting her vision, she glared up at him. "Well, I don't believe that!"

He stared at her, a mixture of hurt and regret glimmering in his azure blue eyes. "You really don't trust me at all, do you?"

Her gut knotted. Everything that had just been within reach—love, marriage, family—splintered and dissolved.

She shook her head miserably. "I don't trust the system, Dan." She emphasized the difference.

"I'm sorry about that," he said softly. Coming closer, he took her in his arms despite her obvious resistance. He stroked a hand through her hair, reminding her that in the last few weeks, he'd not just loved her in ways she had never imagined possible, but that he'd had her back the way no one ever had before.

His gaze and touch gentled all the more. "I'm sorry you had a tough time as a kid." He nuzzled her hair. Brought her even closer. "But what happened to you in

Arizona," he continued tenderly, "has nothing to do with what goes on here in Laramie County."

If only she could believe that, Kelly thought wistfully. Her heart reaching out for him even as her rational mind pushed him away.

But she—and her mother—had been caught up in the system multiple times when she was a child, and found it nothing but a vicious circle.

And if Dan couldn't—wouldn't—understand that. If he didn't believe her? What kind of future could they have?

Conflicted, confused, she splayed her hands across his chest and pushed him away.

He let her go.

Maybe because he knew this had to be said, and it would be so much easier to do so if they weren't touching or linked in any way.

Oblivious to her pain, he continued in that firm resolute tone she knew so well. "I have a responsibility here, Kelly, as a law officer who is charged with protecting the citizens of this county. And when I see a situation like this, where a child potentially could be in jeopardy, I have to report it and get help for them."

"No," she replied equably, "you don't. Not if we handle it on our own."

"You're really suggesting I do this?" Contempt warred with cool.

She told herself he had a right to be angry and upset, too. They all did. It was one hell of a difficult situation. "Yes."

"For how long?" he bit out.

She didn't know the answer to that, any more than she knew anything about caring for someone who had lupus. But she could figure it out, given just a little bit of time!

His lips forming a sober, downward curve, he stepped

closer. "Say we do as Sharon is insisting and drive her home tonight—against medical advice. What then?" he argued. "Do we leave her at her house—which is what I imagine she will want—when you and I both know she should still be in the hospital? Do we leave Shoshanna alone with her mom, who could possibly collapse again at any time, thereby further traumatizing the child? Or do you and I take Shoshanna over to your place, and leave Sharon at her home by herself?" He paused to let his contentious words sink in. 'What happens if Sharon is alone and her condition worsens and she's too ill to call for help?"

It was almost too much to think about. Kelly shoved her hands through her hair. "Maybe both of them can come home with me."

His frown deepened. "And if Sharon doesn't agree to that?"

Which, knowing her very independent friend, seemed likely? Kelly exhaled. "I agree there are no easy answers here."

Dan studied her. "Don't you see? Any temporary resolution that you and I came up with now would only make the situation worse?"

And yet…

Kelly flushed under his steady regard. "It can't be worse than running the risk of Shoshanna being put in foster care."

He released a short breath and came even closer. "I disagree." He got his phone out again.

Misery engulfed her anew. "Dan, if you do this, it's the end of us. I mean it."

He turned a disillusioned glance her way, his hurt and dismay evident.

She hurt, too, but it was only a fraction what they would feel if they continued recklessly down this path.

He recoiled as if she had slapped him. "Then, it's over." He walked away.

And just like that, her life fell apart once again.

Chapter Fifteen

"Taking down the pen?"

Dan looked up to see his mother crossing the yard. He was glad to see her and yet wary too. Because if there was anyone who would encourage him to look into the deepest recesses of his heart and deal with his true feelings, it was her.

He ripped off another section of mesh fencing. "I don't need it anymore."

Rachel watched him roll it up and put it into the bed of the battered old pickup he'd decided to keep, just for chores such as these. "Know what you're going to put in its place?"

He'd been thinking new grass. A swing set. And climbing fort. Maybe a shade tree or two. Or a nice patio, with a fire pit for winter and a grill and picnic table for summer.

With the claw end of his hammer, he worked loose another section. Aware that those plans, like the rest of his life, had gone all to hell. "I don't know yet."

Rachel followed him. "I heard you gave away the goats."

Dan grimaced as he tore loose another section of mesh. "Rehomed them."

Rachel scoffed. "I'm sure *they* are better off."

Dan grunted. "As opposed to?"

His mother assisted in the rolling up of that section. "A certain someone and her three children?"

He turned to avoid another probing look. "We were never a thing, Mom, not really."

"Hmm."

The presumption rankled.

"What do you mean, 'hmm'?" he bit out.

"It looked like you were very much involved the evening you two came over to borrow <u>the</u> tables and chairs."

Dan pushed aside the bittersweet memory. No doubt, those few weeks he'd spent with Kelly and the kids had been the most amazing of his entire life. Too bad they hadn't lasted.

He yanked a post out of the ground and tossed it into the pile of soon to be recycled materials. "Yeah, well, looks can be deceiving."

Rachel followed him back to the partially torn-down fence. "So what happened?"

Dan figured he might as well confide in someone. "Kelly asked me to look the other way when it came to reporting something, and I couldn't do it."

"So," Rachel surmised, understanding, "it was shades of Belinda all over again."

Heart twisting with pain, he nodded.

Rachel came closer. "With a pretty big difference, though. Belinda was working to preserve her ill-gotten family money and avoid criminal indictment. It's my understanding that Kelly was trying to protect a friend from being separated from her three-year-old daughter, the way she and her mother were when she was a child."

"Except it wasn't necessary," Dan countered irritably.

Rachel shrugged. "So she made a mistake and underestimated you. Have you spoken with her about it?"

"No."

She studied him closely. "Why not?"

Hurt battled frustration. Dan wiped the sweat from his brow. "She doesn't trust me, Mom. What kind of relationship can you have without trust?"

"None." Rachel paused, then continued gently, "Of course, trust is a two-way street."

He was listening.

"So is forgiveness."

Guilt flooded him.

Rachel edged nearer still, maternal kindness in her eyes. "Life is full of challenges, Dan. For everyone, all the time. And those challenges are always weathered better when you share them with someone you love."

KELLY WALKED INTO Sharon's living room late Friday. It had been almost a week since the two women had seen each other, although they had talked frequently on the phone. "You look good." The butterfly rash on her face had almost faded completely. Although she was still periodically spiking fevers, the gastrointestinal symptoms had eased, and the stiffness in her joints was barely noticeable.

"Thank you. I'm feeling much better now that I'm on the proper medication again. And of course it helps having home health aides here as much or as little as Shoshanna and I need them."

"I heard Mitzy Martin arranged all of that for you."

Sharon gestured for Kelly to sit down. "And so much more. Seriously, I owe Dan a debt of gratitude. For calling in social services to talk to me before I left the hospital." She shook her head in regret. "I really thought I was doing the right thing, hiding the return of my illness and swearing my daughter to secrecy. I thought I was protecting Shoshanna. Instead, I was putting a burden on her no three-year-old should ever have to carry."

She poured them both a cup of green tea. "But thanks to the intervention of DCFS, and the compromise Mitzy Martin worked out between the doctors and me, I was able to safely return home that very night. With home nursing help to care for me and watch over Shoshanna, I can do all the required medical testing needed to determine a proper course of treatment on an outpatient basis."

Laramie County DCFS had indeed worked miracles. Just as Dan had said they would.

"What about your job?" Kelly asked.

Sharon breathed a sigh of relief. "I resigned my position as financial manager at the dealership. It's too stressful. There are too many long hours."

"Are you going to be okay financially?"

Sharon nodded. "I have enough resources to get me through the interim. And a friend of Mitzy's put me in touch with a recruiter who is going to help me find a work at home finance or accounting job when I'm able to go back, which should be in a couple of weeks."

She paused to sip her tea. "What about you and Dan? How are the two of you?"

Misery engulfed Kelly's heart. She ran her finger around the rim of the cup. "We're not really seeing each other anymore."

Sharon looked as unhappy about that as Kelly felt. "Are you sure it's something that can't be fixed?"

Up to now, Kelly had only been on the receiving end of betrayal. It devastated her to admit that she had dished out that level of pain, too. When it was the last thing she had ever intended.

Regretfully, she shook her head, said, "I didn't trust him, Sharon. Instead, I gave him an ultimatum. I said if he called in social services it was going to be the end of us."

Sharon paused sympathetically. "That's understandable, though, given what you went through when you were a kid."

The green tea, usually so soothing, settled like lead in the pit of Kelly's stomach. If only there were do-overs in life! "I still should have trusted him."

"Have you told him that?"

"You don't know him. Not like I do. When something or someone doesn't fit in his life—" like the other Laramie women he'd dated, *like me* "—he has no problem walking away. Moving on."

"What the two of you had is different, Kelly."

Was it?

Kelly wished it were that simple. She shook her head. "You didn't see the look on his face." The look that had said he would never, ever forgive her for throwing down that ultimatum.

The look that said their relationship just wasn't working. Not the way it should.

Sharon set her cup aside. "Okay, maybe I didn't see his expression at that particular moment. But I saw the way he looked at you and the kids plenty of other times. He cares about you."

And I care about him. So very much.

Yet she still worried it was too late.

"Kelly, take it from me," Sharon continued fiercely. "You may get only one chance in this life to be with the man of your dreams. And even if you do," she said, her voice breaking a little, "it can be gone in a flash, the way my love with my late husband was."

Kelly's eyes welled up, too. "So what are you saying?" she asked hoarsely.

"We're all human. We all make bad decisions in the heat of the moment." She paused to let her words sink in. "It doesn't mean we can't go back and at least try to make things right."

KELLY THOUGHT ABOUT Sharon's words, the rest of the day. By morning of the next day, she knew what she had to do. So she got a babysitter, and then drove out to Bowie Creek Ranch to talk to Dan just as she had a few weeks before.

A building-supply delivery truck was just leaving as she turned in the drive.

Dan was out in the yard, where the goat pen had once stood, looking over enormous piles of building materials. Stone and brick. Bags of cement. Lumber, of all sizes, lengths and widths. Big buckets of hardware and hinges.

Whatever he had going on, it was quite a project.

And he was quite a man, standing there, as solid and strong and invincible as he had always been. And yet so heartrendingly scrumptious and inviting, too.

His sable hair was tousled as if he'd been running his hands through it all morning, and it gleamed in the sunlight. A light blue T-shirt stretched across his shoulders, contrasting nicely with his suntanned skin, and nicely delineating his muscular arms, taut pecs and abs. Worn jeans and construction boots did equally interesting things for his lower half.

As he turned toward her, his expression was initially maddeningly inscrutable, giving her no clue as to what he was thinking.

But that didn't matter, she told herself fiercely. She knew what was in her heart now, and they could build on that.

Gathering her courage, she emerged from her car and

shut the door behind her. As they faced off, his gaze took in her floral cap-sleeved sundress, with the flaring knee-length skirt. The fancy boots, and the lightweight lacy cardigan she'd tied about her waist.

She'd worried the care she had taken getting ready to approach him might be too much. Judging by the appreciative tilt of his lips and the hopeful gleam in his eyes, it was not.

Thank heavens for that.

Still smiling, he strode toward her, not stopping until they'd met exactly halfway. The crinkles around his eyes deepened. "You're not supposed to be out here just yet," he drawled, a familiar twinkle in his azure blue eyes. "Not until I complete a few things. Although, I am aware that my, um, enthusiasm could jinx things."

So he'd had time to reconsider their breakup, too. "Jinx things," Kelly repeated, flushing beneath his tender scrutiny. "Like what?"

His voice dropped a sexy notch, his gaze devouring her from head to toe. "Us."

"There's still an 'us'?"

"Oh, yeah," he said with the quiet confidence she loved, taking her all the way into his arms. He threaded one hand through her hair, wrapped the other about her waist. He jerked in a rough breath. "Even though, this last week, we've been temporarily put on hold."

Kelly splayed her hands across his chest; the rapid beat of his heart matched hers. "By my lunacy," she admitted as tears of happiness misted her eyes and clogged her throat.

"And mine," he said gruffly.

The relief inside her built.

Her heart pounding like a wild thing in her chest, she snuggled against him, taking all the heat and strength he had to give. "I'm sorry, Dan," she whispered emotionally. "So sorry I gave you an ultimatum." She tipped her head back to better see into his eyes. "I should have trusted you when you said Laramie was different, and that you wouldn't let anything bad happen."

He lifted her hand, kissed the back of it, then held it against his chest, over his still-racing heart. "Why couldn't you?" he asked thickly.

The tears she'd been holding back spilled over her lashes and ran down her cheeks. Her voice caught. "Because I was scared to put my trust in anyone but myself. Scared if I did and it all blew up, it wouldn't just be me getting hurt this time, it would be my kids, too." She leaned in. "And I didn't want them to live with the kind of heart-wrenching disappointment I suffered as a child."

He tightened his grip on her. "And now…?"

"I've realized that while I thought I was being a good parent and protecting them, I've actually been short-changing them. The truth is," she admitted, while he stroked a hand through her hair, "I'm never going to find true happiness unless I open myself up to all the possibilities, and neither will my kids."

She wreathed her arms around his broad shoulders. "Yes, loving you will always be a risk, but it's also one that promises the greatest reward of all, and I do love you, Dan," she revealed in a voice that trembled with all she felt. "With all my heart and soul." Letting him see how much, she rose on tiptoe and kissed him, deeply, sweetly.

"I love you, too," he said in the rough-hewn voice she loved so much, kissing her again. He held her so close their hearts pounded in unison.

He shook his head. "Which is why I never should have walked away the way I did that night."

The depth of his regret matched hers. "Why did you?"

He drew a deep breath, his eyes never leaving hers. Letting her know in that moment that she wasn't the only one who had been doing some soul-searching. "I was afraid to let myself believe that our feelings for each other could survive a test." He put his arm around her shoulders and led her toward the house. "So instead of giving us both a chance to weather the difficulty together, I did exactly what I accused you of doing—" his lips tightened ruefully "—and cut ties at the first sign of hardship." He opened the door and drew her across the threshold. "I was wrong to do that, Kelly."

She settled on the sectional next to him. "We both were."

Grinning, he pulled her onto his lap. "Because if we're ever going to be as happy as we are meant to be, we have to accept that there will be challenges," he said, cuddling her close. "And when we encounter them, we have to stick together. And remember that forgiveness and understanding are key."

Amen to that, Kelly thought, turning to face him, so she straddled his lap.

He rubbed his thumb across her lower lip. Continued looking deep into her eyes. "So…truce?"

"Absolutely." Grinning, Kelly looped her hands about his shoulders. "As long as we can pick up where we left off…"

"Actually," he said, an equally mischievous smile crossing his face, "I want a little more than that."

The edges of her broken heart mending, she waited. Ready to give him whatever he wanted and needed. From this day forward.

"I want you to marry me, Kelly," he told her with fierce intensity. "I want you and me and the kids and Shep to be the family we're meant to be."

She couldn't have asked for more. Happiness flooded

her, heart and soul. She pressed her lips to his. "I think I can live with that."

He kissed her again, even more deeply this time.

She melted against him, glad she had found the love of her life at long last. "I think I can *very happily* live with that."

He chuckled and folded her close. "So can I, sweetheart. So can I."

... with his...

Epilogue

Father's Day, one year later...

"You can't get up just yet." Kelly put a hand to the center of Dan's chest and pushed him back against the pillows.

Dan winced as the racket on the first floor of the Bowie Creek ranch house escalated. Wild giggling ensued, followed by occasional arguing. As much as he loved hanging out with his beautiful wife, duty called. Prepared to take on the daddy responsibilities he loved so much, he tossed back the covers. "I think I'd better go and see."

Kelly grinned. "I promise you. It's handled."

Something else fell or was dropped. Maybe a utensil? Definitely not glass. Dan frowned. "It doesn't sound like it's handled."

"It is, I promise." Kelly rose gracefully, looking as sexy as ever in a floral nightgown and matching sleep cardigan. She pirouetted away from him, then turned back, just enough, to send him a playful glance over her slender shoulder. "Or at least it will be when I get down there again."

Her sweet, sultry voice filled him with contentment. He let his glance drift over her. How was it possible, he wondered, that she got more lovely with every passing day? He, more deeply in love?

Something else fell with a clatter. From the sound of it, probably another utensil of some sort. "You're sure?" he said.

Shimmering with joy, she came back long enough to kiss him. "Yes! Now stay put. And when you hear thundering footsteps on the stairs, you better at least look like you're just waking up!"

Having received his orders, he gave her a mock salute. "Yes, ma'am."

Her soft, melodic laugh filled the room. "It will be worth it, I promise."

Dan was sure it would. And when a cacophony of sound preceded the kids up the stairs fifteen minutes later, his assumption was confirmed.

"Surprise, Daddy! Happy Father's Day!" The pajama-clad triplets burst through the door, bringing with them an assortment of paper cups, plates and plastic utensils.

Kelly carried an oversize breakfast tray that held a towering stack of toast. Orange juice and iced coffee in clear-lidded carafes. And enough bacon, scrambled eggs and hash browns to feed all of them.

"Look at the breakfast Mommy and us fixed for you!" Matthew pointed out.

"We put the butter on the toast after it cooled," Michael said.

"Yeah, and the blackberry jam, because it's your favorite," Michelle explained.

A lump grew in Dan's throat.

"It's wonderful," he said, his heart filling as his family surrounded him on the bed, picnic style. Kelly doled out the food, and the kids chattered nonstop while they ate. About the big event early in the spring—his and Kelly's wedding, which they all had participated in, much to the hopelessly romantic Michelle's delight. And the skiing honeymoon for five—to Colorado—that had followed.

From there, the conversation flowed to their friend Shoshanna, whose mother was in remission and doing great again. Then they had to talk about the pet goats they still visited from time to time. The fun they had in preschool. And how much they liked life on the ranch they now all called home.

Finally, Matthew asked, inquisitive as always, "Daddy, do you think we can get a new puppy to go with the new baby growing in Mommy's tummy?"

Michael pointed out, "We already got one new puppy. Last year. So Shep wouldn't be so lonely, on account of the goats leaving."

"Yes, but if we got another puppy, then we'd have three dogs and three kids," Matthew calculated persuasively.

"Or," Michelle chimed in, not about to be left out of such an important decision, "we could get a cat or a hamster, or maybe even a pet llama."

Looking as if it were all she could do not to groan aloud at that suggestion, Kelly put a hand over her barely there baby bump. "Actually, guys, I think that by the time Christmas gets here and the babies are born, we're all going to be too busy to get any new pets for a while."

The kids had to think about that.

So did Dan, as Kelly's word choice sunk in. "Babies?" he echoed, aware what that meant. He focused on the excited sparkle in Kelly's eyes, still feeling a little stunned. "We're having *twins*?"

The flush in Kelly's cheeks deepened, making her look even more gorgeous. "Um, actually...triplets!"

"Three babies!" Dan exalted.

Excited, the kids let out a cheer.

Hugs and kisses were exchanged all around.

Thrilled, the kids went to get dressed, so they could go outside to play in the now very family-friendly backyard.

Taking advantage of their moment alone, Dan moved the tray aside and opened his arms. Kelly slid into them. "Happy?" she asked, laying her head on his shoulder.

He nodded, his heart overflowing as he realized that dreaming big when it came to the two of them hadn't been so far out of left field after all. "More than you could ever know," he confided softly.

Threading his hands through her hair, he tilted her head up to his and kissed her with all the love he had in his heart.

Tenderness flowed between them, as potent as ever.

"Me, too," she whispered gratefully, kissing him back. Once and then again.

Drawing apart, they shared a triumphant laugh. Realizing, as did she, that all their dreams—and more—had come true, Dan drawled, "Seems like we're going to be filling up this seven-bedroom, seven-bath house and eight-passenger vehicle after all!"

* * * * *

COMING SOON!

We really hope you enjoyed reading this book. If
you're looking for more romance, be sure to head
to the shops when new books are available on

Thursday
28th June

To see which titles are coming soon, please visit
millsandboon.co.uk

MILLS & BOON

Coming next month

REUNITED AT THE ALTAR
Kate Hardy

Cream roses.

Brad had bought her cream roses.

Had he remembered that had been her wedding bouquet, Abigail wondered, a posy of half a dozen cream roses they'd bought last-minute at the local florist? Or had he just decided that roses were the best flowers to make an apology and those were the first ones he'd seen? She raked a shaking hand through her hair. It might not have been the best idea to agree to have dinner with Brad tonight.

Then again, he'd said he wanted a truce for Ruby's sake, and they needed to talk.

But seeing him again had stirred up all kinds of emotions she'd thought she'd buried a long time ago. She'd told herself that she was over her ex and could move on. The problem was, Bradley Powell was still the most attractive man she'd ever met – those dark, dark eyes; the dark hair that she knew curled outrageously when it was wet; that sense of brooding about him. She'd never felt that same spark with anyone else she'd dated. She knew she hadn't been fair to the few men who'd asked her out; she really shouldn't have compared them to her first love, because how could they ever match up to him?

She could still remember the moment she'd fallen in love with Brad. She and Ruby had been revising for their English exams together in the garden, and Brad had come out to join them, wanting a break from his physics revision. Somehow he'd ended up reading Benedick's speeches while she'd read Beatrice's.

'I do love nothing in the world so well as you: is that not strange?'

She'd glanced up from her text and met his gaze, and a surge of heat had spun through her. He was looking at her as if it was the first time he'd ever seen her. As if she was the only living thing in the world apart from himself. As if the rest of the world had just melted away...

Continue reading

REUNITED AT THE ALTAR
Kate Hardy

Available next month
www.millsandboon.co.uk

LET'S TALK
Romance

For exclusive extracts, competitions
and special offers, find us online:

[f] facebook.com/millsandboon

[◎] @millsandboonuk

[🐦] @millsandboon

Or get in touch on 0844 844 1351*

For all the latest titles coming soon, visit
millsandboon.co.uk/nextmonth